How to use your Sna

This 'An Inspector Calls' Snap Revision ~~~~ ur
Edexcel English Literature exam. It is di
easily find help for the bits you find tricky. ~~~ .d
to know for the exam:

Plot: what happens in the play?

Setting and Context: what periods, places, events and attitudes are relevant to understanding the play?

Characters: who are the main characters, how are they presented, and how do they change?

Themes: what ideas does the author explore in the play, and how are they shown?

The Exam: what kinds of question will come up in your exam, and how can you get top marks?

To help you get ready for your exam, each two-page topic includes the following:

Key Quotations to Learn
Short quotations to memorise that will allow you to analyse in the exam and boost your grade.

Summary
A recap of the most important points covered in the topic.

Sample Analysis
An example of the kind of analysis that the examiner will be looking for.

Quick Test
A quick-fire test to check you can remember the main points from the topic.

Exam Practice
A short writing task so you can practise applying what you've covered in the topic.

Glossary
A handy list of words you will find useful when revising 'An Inspector Calls' with easy-to-understand definitions.

AUTHOR:
IAN KIRBY

ebook

To access the ebook version of this Snap Revision Text Guide, visit

collins.co.uk/ebooks
and follow the step-by-step instructions.

Published by Collins
An imprint of HarperCollins*Publishers*
1 London Bridge Street
London SE1 9GF

HarperCollins*Publishers*
1st Floor, Watermarque Building,
Ringsend Road, Dublin 4, Ireland

ISBN 978-0-00-835301-8

First published 2019

10 9 8 7 6 5

British Library Cataloguing in Publication Data.
A CIP record of this book is available from the
British Library.

Commissioning Editor: Fiona McGlade
Project Managers: Shelley Teasdale and
  Richard Toms
Author: Ian Kirby
Proofreader: Lauren Murray
Typesetting: Mark Steward and QBS Learning
Cover designers: Kneath Associates and
  Sarah Duxbury
Production: Karen Nulty
Printed and bound in the UK using 100%
Renewable Electricity at CPI Group (UK) Ltd

ACKNOWLEDGEMENTS
Quotations from An Inspector Calls taken
from An Inspector Calls and Other Plays by
J.B. Priestley, 2001, London. An Inspector Calls
copyright 1947 by J.B. Priestley. Reproduced by
permission of Penguin Books Ltd.

The author and publisher are grateful to the
copyright holders for permission to use quoted
materials and images.

Every effort has been made to trace copyright
holders and obtain their permission for the
use of copyright material. The author and
publisher will gladly receive information
enabling them to rectify any error or omission
in subsequent editions. All facts are correct at
time of going to press.

MIX
Paper from
responsible source

FSC
www.fsc.org   FSC™ C007454

This book is produced from independently
certified FSC™ paper to ensure responsible
forest management.

For more information visit:
www.harpercollins.co.uk/green

Contents

Act 1 (part 1)

You must be able to: understand what happens at the start of the play.

The setting

The play is set in 1912, in the fictional industrial city of Brumley, North Midlands.

The opening stage directions reveal that the play takes place in the large suburban house of a wealthy businessman.

What is the situation?

The Birling family – Mr Arthur Birling, Mrs Sybil Birling and their two children, Eric and Sheila – have just finished dinner. There is a happy atmosphere.

The Birlings' guest is Gerald Croft, Sheila's wealthy fiancé, and they are all celebrating the couple's engagement.

Who are the characters?

The audience are briefly introduced to all the characters but the focus is on Arthur Birling.

After congratulating the young couple, he makes a speech about 1912's social and political climate.

He and Gerald are then left alone for a while and he talks of his social aspirations.

It is made clear that Gerald and the Birlings are pleased with their lives and see themselves as good people.

When Eric returns to the room, Mr Birling continues to talk to the young men about his experience of the world but is interrupted by the doorbell.

What changes the situation?

Inspector Goole arrives and the audience are told about the suicide of a young woman called Eva Smith.

Despite Mr Birling's status, the Inspector is confident, abrupt and mysterious.

Mr Birling sacked Eva from his factory two years ago, in September 1910. She led a group of girls to ask for a pay-rise of two-and-a-half shillings a week. This turned into an unsuccessful **strike**, after which the ringleaders, including Eva, were sacked.

Mr Birling finds himself defending his actions and Gerald supports him.

Hearing Eva's story, Eric feels sorry for her, which causes him to argue with his father.

The Inspector is clearly on Eva's side and this angers Mr Birling. He tries to intimidate the Inspector, which he ignores.

At this point, Sheila innocently enters the room.

Key Quotations to Learn

Arthur Birling: 'It's one of the happiest nights of my life'

Gerald: '[*laughs*] You seem to be a nice well-behaved family'

Inspector: 'I'd like some information, if you don't mind'

Summary

- The Birlings are celebrating and they are very happy.
- The Inspector interrupts to discuss Eva Smith's suicide.
- Eva was sacked two years ago from Mr Birling's factory.
- The discussion of the suicide causes conflict on stage between Mr Birling, Eric and the Inspector.

Questions

QUICK TEST
1. Who are the four members of the Birling family?
2. What is the family celebrating?
3. Why does Inspector Goole arrive at the Birlings' house?
4. How is Eva Smith linked to Arthur Birling?
5. What different opinions do the characters have about Arthur's treatment of Eva?

EXAM PRACTICE
Using one or more of the 'Key Quotations to Learn', write a paragraph exploring the significance of the family's contentment at the start of the play.

Act 1 (part 2)

You must be able to: understand what happens in the second half of Act 1.

How does the focus shift to Sheila?

Sheila is upset by the news of the girl's suicide and the Inspector reveals that the case involves more than just Mr Birling.

The Inspector gives some background to Eva's life and her situation. Sheila agrees with him that the girl led a pitiful life and needed **compassion**.

The Inspector tells of how Eva took a job at Milwards in December 1910 but she was then sacked in January 1911 after a complaint by a customer. Sheila recognises the girl's picture and runs out of the room upset.

When she returns, Sheila admits that it is her fault that the girl was sacked.

She explains that she was in a bad mood and felt the girl was laughing at her. She also admits she was jealous of Eva's prettiness. She is clearly upset but partly for herself rather than just about Eva's death.

How does the focus shift to Gerald?

When Sheila leaves the room upset, Mr Birling departs to speak to her and his wife.

Eric and Gerald are left with the Inspector. Eric gets angry and tries to leave the room but the Inspector insists that he stays.

After Sheila returns and confesses, the Inspector tells the three young people that Eva Smith changed her name to Daisy Renton. From Gerald's reaction, he is clearly disturbed by this news.

The Inspector and Eric go to the drawing room to speak to Mr and Mrs Birling, leaving Sheila and Gerald alone.

Sheila realises that Gerald was having an affair with Daisy during the previous spring/summer of 1911.

Gerald thinks it can be hidden but Sheila realises that the Inspector knows everything already.

The Inspector returns to the dining room.

Key Quotations to Learn

Sheila: 'What do you mean by saying that? You talk as if we were responsible – '

Sheila: '[*miserably*] So I'm really responsible?'

Gerald: 'So – for God's sake – don't say anything to the Inspector'

Summary

- Sheila feels sorry for Eva Smith.
- Sheila confesses that she complained about the girl and got her sacked from Milwards.
- Eva Smith changed her name to Daisy Renton.
- Gerald admits to Sheila that he had an affair with Daisy.

Questions

QUICK TEST

1. What does Sheila feel for Eva Smith when she first hears about her sacking and her suicide?
2. Why did Sheila get Eva sacked from Milwards?
3. What is significant about the reasons for Sheila being upset?
4. Who reacts strangely to the news that Eva changed her named to Daisy Renton?
5. What do we find out about Daisy's life during the spring/summer of 1911?

EXAM PRACTICE

Using one or more of the 'Key Quotations to Learn', write a paragraph exploring the importance of responsibility in the play.

Act 2 (part 1)

You must be able to: understand what happens in the first half of Act 2.

How is Mrs Birling presented?

Continuing from the end of Act 1, Gerald tries to get Sheila to leave so he can hide his involvement but she refuses.

As the Inspector talks about their joint responsibility, Mrs Birling enters very confidently. Sheila is instantly worried as she, Gerald and Arthur had all behaved the same way.

Mrs Birling behaves in a **superior** manner, referring to Eva's lower class status, talking down to Sheila, acting grandly in front of the Inspector and referring to her husband's high status in the community. Despite this, the Inspector remains calm and blunt when speaking to her.

When Sheila reveals that Eric drinks too much, a fact that Gerald confirms, Mrs Birling is shocked and annoyed.

Sheila repeats her warning that her parents are making the situation worse and they are shocked to discover that Gerald knew Eva/Daisy.

How did Gerald know Daisy?

Gerald says he met Daisy in March 1911 in a bar. Sheila's parents don't want her to hear his story but she refuses to leave.

The reality of Daisy's death suddenly hits Gerald and he's visibly distressed.

He describes taking Daisy for a drink. She wanted to talk, having been upset by an encounter with Joe Meggarty (a city councillor who Gerald describes as a **womanising** drunk, which shocks Mrs Birling).

Gerald explains to the Inspector how Daisy had no money and was hungry. He innocently moved her into a friend's apartment and they later became lovers. Mrs Birling is disgusted by his behaviour.

Sheila points out that Gerald should be explaining to her not to the Inspector.

Gerald says that he didn't love Daisy but enjoyed being loved. He broke off the relationship in September 1911. The Inspector reveals that Daisy then went to the seaside; she wrote in her diary that she wanted to be alone to pretend her time with Gerald was continuing.

Gerald asks to go for a walk. Before he leaves, Sheila returns the engagement ring. She says she respects his honesty but they are now both different people.

Key Quotations to Learn

Inspector: 'we'll have to share our guilt'

Mrs Birling: 'Girls of that class'

Gerald: 'All she wanted was to talk – a little friendliness'

Summary

- Gerald still hopes to hide his involvement with Eva/Daisy.
- The Inspector tells Gerald and Sheila that they are all responsible.
- Mrs Birling behaves in a superior way to the Inspector, Gerald and Sheila.
- Gerald reveals the details of his affair with Daisy, and Sheila breaks off the engagement.

Questions

QUICK TEST
1. Why does Gerald want Sheila to leave the room?
2. How does Mrs Birling criticise Eva Smith?
3. How does Mrs Birling behave in front of the Inspector?
4. Why is Sheila worried by her mother's behaviour?
5. What was Gerald's relationship with Daisy like?

EXAM PRACTICE
Using one or more of the 'Key Quotations to Learn', write a paragraph exploring the significance of Eva/Daisy in the play.

Act 2 (part 2)

You must be able to: understand what happens in the second half of Act 2.

What was Mrs Birling's role in Eva Smith's death?

Mrs Birling says she doesn't recognise the photo of Eva. The Inspector and Sheila know she's lying.

The Inspector says that Mrs Birling is a prominent member of the Brumley Women's Charity Organisation and that Eva appealed to the charity two weeks ago.

Sybil reveals that Eva was using the name 'Mrs Birling', which she found insulting and so was instantly **prejudiced** against her.

Mrs Birling states that Eva only had herself to blame and says that it was her duty to use her influence to have the girl's claim refused.

The Inspector reveals that Eva was pregnant but clarifies that it wasn't Gerald's child.

Mrs Birling told the girl to look for the child's father as it was his responsibility. Sheila says her mother's behaviour was horrible, while Arthur suggests that it will look bad on them. In response, she points out that it was Arthur sacking Eva 'which probably began it all'.

How does the focus begin to turn on Eric?

At this point, it has not been made clear that Eric was the father of Eva Smith's child but the audience may be beginning to work it out. Just as Mrs Birling begins to be questioned, there is the sound of Eric leaving the house and the Inspector comments that he will be needed.

As the Inspector continues to question Mrs Birling, he pushes her into criticising the father of the **illegitimate** child. She also calls Eva a liar for claiming the man had offered her money but she thought it was stolen so didn't want to take it.

Mrs Birling refuses to accept any blame, saying it is the girl's fault first and the lover's second. She says the man should be made an example of and accepts that if the girl's story about stolen money is true then the lover is entirely to blame.

Sheila works out Eric's involvement and tries to stop her mother saying any more.

As Mr and Mrs Birling begin to realise the truth, Eric returns to the dining room.

Key Quotations to Learn

Mrs Birling: 'I'm very sorry. But I think she only had herself to blame'

Mrs Birling: 'As if a girl of that sort would ever refuse money!'

Sheila: '[*with sudden alarm*] Mother – stop! – stop!'

Summary

- Eva was pregnant and asked Mrs Birling's charity for help.
- Mrs Birling didn't like the girl and used her influence to have the claim rejected.
- The Inspector manipulates Mrs Birling into stating that the father of Eva's child is entirely to blame for her death.
- The audience and the characters on stage gradually realise that Eric is the father.

Questions

QUICK TEST
1. What immediately turned Mrs Birling against Eva?
2. Does Mrs Birling regret rejecting the girl's claim for charity?
3. How do Sheila and Mr Birling respond differently to the news that Mrs Birling didn't help a pregnant girl who was asking for charity?
4. What did Mrs Birling think the girl was lying about?
5. Why does Sheila try to stop Mrs Birling from criticising the father of Eva's child?

EXAM PRACTICE
Using one or more of the 'Key Quotations to Learn', write a paragraph exploring the importance of prejudice in the play.

Act 3 (part 1)

You must be able to: understand what happens in the first half of Act 3.

How did Eric affect Eva Smith's life?

The story picks up from the end of Act 2 and Eric realises that everyone knows the truth.

The family argue over Eric's drinking and he retells how he met Eva in a bar.

After he turned aggressive, she let him into her flat where they had sex. At this point, Mr Birling orders Sheila to take her mother out of the room.

Eric continues his **confession**. He met Eva again, by accident, and they slept together. Eva revealed that she was pregnant but knew Eric didn't love her. To help the girl, he stole money from Arthur's office but she refused to take it.

How is Mr Birling presented at this point?

Arthur loses his temper several times before Eric's confession: first with the Inspector, who refuses to be intimidated by him, and then with Sheila when she doesn't want to leave the room.

He also shows his aggression during Eric's confession. When Eric points out that some of Birling's supposedly **respectable** friends have affairs, the Inspector has to stop Arthur from interrupting. He has another angry reaction when Eric admits to stealing.

Arthur also comes across badly when Eric explains his poor relationship with his father, feeling that he couldn't have asked him for help.

In addition to this, his reaction is still to cover the events up and avoid public scandal. It is particularly damning when he says he would give thousands of pounds to make the problem go away, showing his **capitalist** values rather than genuine regret.

How does the Inspector make his exit?

When Sheila and Sybil return, the Inspector tells Eric how Eva was rejected by his mother's committee, causing Eric to accuse Sybil of killing Eva and her own grandchild.

The Inspector sums up, telling them they all killed Eva Smith. He goes through the family, one by one, finally reminding Arthur that he destroyed a girl over two-and-a-half shillings.

The Inspector then focuses on the state of the country, pointing out that there are 'millions of Eva Smiths and John Smiths'. Talking to the Birlings (and the audience) he says, 'We are members of one body. We are responsible for each other'. He leaves with a warning that change will have to come.

Key Quotations to Learn

Mr Birling (to Sheila): '[*very sharply*] You heard what I said'

Eric: 'You're not the kind of father a chap could go to when he's in trouble'

Mr Birling (to Eric): '[*furious, intervening*] Why you hysterical young fool – get back – or I'll – '

Inspector: 'We don't live alone. We are members of one body. We are responsible for each other'

Summary

- Eric met Eva and made her pregnant.
- Eric accuses his mother of killing Eva and the baby, and says his father is unapproachable.
- The Inspector reminds the Birlings that they are all responsible for Eva Smith's death.
- The Inspector states his belief that all the members of society need to look after each other.

Questions

QUICK TEST
1. What negative aspects of Eric's character are revealed?
2. Why wouldn't Eva marry Eric?
3. What does Eric accuse his mother of?
4. In what way does Arthur not seem to have changed during the play?
5. What is the Inspector's final message before he leaves?

EXAM PRACTICE
Using one or more of the 'Key Quotations to Learn', write a paragraph exploring the significance of power in the play.

Act 3 (part 2)

You must be able to: understand what happens at the end of the play.

What happens after the Inspector leaves?

Arthur's reaction to the evening's events continues to be fear of the scandal. He also states his belief that he and Sybil can excuse their actions.

Sheila shows more guilt, pointing out that her parents haven't learnt anything and criticising them for not focussing on the actual victim.

Sheila and Sybil begin to suspect that the Inspector wasn't a real police officer. Sheila doesn't think it matters because they still killed Eva Smith. However, Mr and Mrs Birling focus on the possibility of the whole affair remaining private if the police don't actually know.

How does Gerald's return alter things?

When Gerald returns, Arthur tries to stop Sheila from telling him about Eric and Sybil's involvement in Eva's death.

Gerald reveals that the Inspector wasn't a real police officer.

Mr and Mrs Birling are relieved and believe the secret can be kept amongst them. Arthur telephones the chief constable and it is confirmed that Inspector Goole doesn't exist.

While Gerald agrees with Arthur and Sybil, Sheila and Eric still feel guilt for what has happened.

Gerald, Arthur, and Sybil begin to think the whole evening may have been a **hoax**. They ring the infirmary and find there is no dead girl.

How does the play end?

Arthur and Gerald relax and are pleased their bad experience is over. Arthur raises a toast to the family but Sheila and Eric refuse to take part.

Arthur feels that everything is back to normal. He laughs about the evening's events and suggests that Sheila asks Gerald for her engagement ring back. Gerald offers her the ring but she refuses.

Sheila and Eric realise that the others have learnt nothing. She and Eric have been affected by the Inspector's words of warning as he left.

Arthur laughs at his two children as the phone rings. It is the police: a girl has died after swallowing disinfectant and an inspector is on his way.

Key Quotations to Learn

Sheila: 'Everything we said had happened really had happened'

Arthur: '[*heartily*] Nonsense! You'll have a good laugh over it yet'

Sheila: 'You began to learn something. And now you've stopped'

Summary

- Gerald reveals that the Inspector wasn't a real police officer.
- They find out that there is no dead girl at the infirmary.
- Arthur, Sybil and Gerald relax, thinking everything can be covered up and forgotten.
- Sheila and Eric still feel guilty and cannot understand the others' behaviour.
- The play ends with a phone call from the police saying a girl has died and an inspector is on his way to the house.

Questions

QUICK TEST
1. What do Arthur and Sybil focus on after the Inspector leaves?
2. What do Sheila and Eric feel after the Inspector leaves?
3. How do Arthur, Sybil and Gerald feel when they realise that the Inspector wasn't real and that a girl hasn't died?
4. Why do Eric and Sheila feel differently to their parents?
5. How does the play end?

EXAM PRACTICE
Using one or more of the 'Key Quotations to Learn', write a paragraph exploring the significance of age in the play.

Narrative Structure

You must be able to: explain the significance of the different ways Priestley has structured the play.

How does Priestley maintain the dramatic focus?

The play takes place on one evening, with each act opening immediately where the other left off.

The play takes place in one setting – the dining room of the Birlings' house.

The play has one central plot – the events leading to Eva Smith's death.

By taking this very singular approach, Priestley can focus on the drama and **tension** of the situation in order to emphasise his message about society.

To achieve this, the characters' involvements in Eva Smith's death are also dealt with one at a time. Characters not needed leave the stage, allowing Priestley to focus the audience on each person's responsibility.

How does Priestley raise and lower the tension?

To make the play and his social message memorable, Priestley uses the narrative structure to keep the **atmosphere** on stage tense and engaging.

Priestley starts each act by lowering the tension. A relaxed mood is established at the start of the play through the happy family meal, while the different character confessions at the beginning of Acts 2 and 3 lower the tension.

Different family arguments create brief spikes in tension, as does the way the Inspector comes into **conflict** with other characters.

At the end of the first two acts, Priestley raises the tension to a climax and includes a **cliffhanger**.

Act 1 ends with the unravelling of Sheila and Gerald's engagement, while the **climax** of Act 2 is even greater with Sybil and Arthur realising the truth about Eric.

Why does Priestley include the twist at the end?

When the Inspector leaves, the play seems to be over.

This trick by Priestley allows the audience to see whether the individual characters have learned anything or changed in any way. It also gives them time to judge each character's attitude to the social questions that Priestley has raised during the play through the character of the Inspector.

The play finally ends on a memorable cliffhanger, ensuring that the audience will question what they have seen and think more about the play's message.

Key Quotations to Learn

Sheila: 'And I hate to think how much he knows that we don't know yet. You'll see. You'll see' (Act 1)

Arthur: '[*thunderstruck*] My God! But – look here – ' (Act 2)

'[*As they stare guiltily and dumbfounded, the curtain falls*]' (Act 3)

Summary

- Priestley uses a simple narrative structure (one plot, one set, one evening) in order to focus his social message.
- The drama is intensified by dealing with each character's guilt one by one, and removing them from the stage when they aren't needed.
- To make the play memorable, Priestley raises and lowers the tension throughout.
- Cliffhangers are used at the end of each act to keep the audience thinking about the events on stage.

Questions

QUICK TEST
1. In what way is the narrative structure of the play quite simple?
2. What narrative technique is used at the end of each act?
3. What things raise and lower the tension during the play?
4. What is Priestley trying to get the audience to focus on and think about?

EXAM PRACTICE
Using one or more of the 'Key Quotations to Learn', write a paragraph exploring the importance of mystery in the play.

Class and Politics

You must be able to: understand the concept of class and the political ideas that are explored in the play.

What is meant by class?

This is a way of grouping different people in society according to their social status and how wealthy they are.

The most familiar labels are upper, middle and working class.

The upper class are seen as having the most money and status in society. This group of people are usually born into an old, established family who own a lot of land and property, rather than gaining wealth through running a business. They often don't need to work. Upper class families would often be linked to a title such as Lord, Sir or Duke. In the play, Gerald is upper class; his parents are Sir George and Lady Croft, who Arthur refers to as 'an old county family – landed people'.

The middle class are people who have recently earned a lot of money. They are usually well-educated with a good profession (such as doctors and lawyers) but can be anyone who has become wealthy through hard work. They are home-owners and aspire to having more money and social status. The Birlings are presented as a middle-class family, having made a lot of money through Arthur's business.

Some of the middle classes are disliked by the upper classes because they have the same amount of money but don't have the same "breeding", meaning they aren't brought up to speak, behave and dress in the strict way that the upper classes see as respectable. This links to Arthur being aware that Lady Croft feels Gerald could have become engaged to someone "better" than Sheila.

The working class are the poorest in society. They work for others, rather than being the bosses, and their wages are fairly low. They are linked to manual labour. The working class also includes the unemployed as they need work to survive. Eva Smith is a good example of a working-class person; she has a job in a factory and, once she is unemployed, has no way to pay for food or rent.

What is capitalism?

Capitalism is a right-wing political belief in individual gain through hard work and a focus on profit. Capitalists accept that, for this to happen, there will always be people in society who are much better off than others.

Birling is a capitalist and talks happily about 'steadily increasing prosperity'. He disagrees with workers asking for more money and sacks Eva Smith and others for going on strike to try to achieve better wages.

What is socialism?

Socialism is a left-wing political belief in greater equality and fairness for all, especially the poorest and most needy in society. Socialists believe working class people should have more of a say in government and that wealth should be more evenly shared amongst the classes.

The Inspector represents socialist values, believing that people like Eva Smith should be better paid and, if they fall on difficult times, supported financially. He feels the poor are used or **exploited** in order to make the middle classes richer. When talking about the number of people in a similar position to Eva Smith, he adds, 'If there weren't, the factories and warehouses wouldn't know where to look for cheap labour. Ask your father'.

Summary

- Society can be divided into upper, middle and working class. In the play, these classes are represented by the Crofts, the Birlings and Eva Smith.
- The term capitalism refers to individual wealth through hard work. This links to Birling.
- Socialism refers to sharing wealth and looking after poorer people in society. This links to the Inspector.

Questions

QUICK TEST

1. In the play, which character is linked to the upper class?
2. Which characters are middle class?
3. What class is Eva Smith?
4. Is Arthur Birling presented as a capitalist or a socialist? How can you tell?

EXAM PRACTICE

In Act 1, Arthur says to Gerald:

'I have an idea that your mother – Lady Croft – while she doesn't object to my girl – feels you might have done better for yourself socially – [...] No Gerald, that's all right. Don't blame her. She comes from an old county family – landed people and so forth – and so it's only natural. But what I wanted to say is – there's a fair chance that I might find my way into the next Honours List. Just a knighthood, of course'.

Relating your ideas to the social context, write a paragraph explaining how Arthur is presented as having higher social aspirations and why he might want this.

J.B. Priestley and 1945

You must be able to: understand how the play's meaning has been shaped by the author's life and the time in which he was writing.

Who was J.B. Priestley and how did his life affect his play?

John Boynton Priestley was born in 1894.

Although not as wealthy as the Birlings in his play, his was also a middle-class **suburban** family.

He left school at 16, took a job as a junior clerk, and began writing in his spare time.

He fought in the First World War (1914–1918) and spent many months in hospital after being badly injured. During the war, he would have fought side by side with all kinds of men regardless of their class.

After the war, Britain and many other countries were plunged into economic **depression**, with widespread poverty and a rise of political extremism. Priestley was influenced by his father's socialist views and wanted the world to become a more equal place.

By the 1930s, he was a successful writer. During the Second World War (1939–1945), Priestley was a radio broadcaster and his programme was very popular. He shared his socialist views and his hopes for a better Britain with listeners until the show was taken off air (because the government thought it too left-wing). These views appear throughout the play via the voice of the Inspector.

Priestley wrote *An Inspector Calls* in 1945. He continued his career as a playwright, novelist, essayist and political commentator until his death in 1984.

How does the time the play was written affect the play?

The two world wars were major contributors to the gradual erosion of Britain's strict class and gender divisions.

At war, men of different classes fought side by side despite any preconceived prejudices. At home, women kept the country running by taking on jobs they had not previously been encouraged to do.

By the 1920s, the Labour Party had grown out of different trade union and socialist movements to become the main opposition party to the Conservatives. The Labour Party had formed minority and coalition governments before and during the war but swept to power with a landslide victory in 1945.

It was this government that established the **welfare state**, introduced the National Health Service and promoted new housing estates where people of different classes would live side by side. However, the country could not change overnight and socialists saw that there was still a lot of work to do.

First performed in 1946, *An Inspector Calls* would have taken an audience back to 1912 and a very different Britain with very different values. It reminded them of the past in order to praise the present and keep pushing for further changes to achieve complete equality.

Summary

- J.B. Priestley grew up in the early 1900s and developed strong socialist beliefs.
- The two world wars began to change society by breaking down the rigid class system.
- The writing of the play coincided with the popularity of left-wing views in Britain.
- *An Inspector Calls* reminds its audience of a very different Britain.

Questions

QUICK TEST
1. How do Priestley's ideas appear through the character of the Inspector?
2. How might Priestley's wartime experiences have helped to shape his socialist principles?
3. How did the post-Second World War Labour government try to make Britain a more equal place?

EXAM PRACTICE
In Act 1, Arthur Birling says, 'We employers at last are coming together to see that our interests – and the interests of Capital – are properly protected. And we're in for a time of steadily increasing prosperity'.

Relating your ideas to the historical context, write a paragraph explaining how Birling's 1912 views might have seemed outdated when the play was first performed in 1946.

The Midlands, 1912

You must be able to: link the events of the play to its setting.

What were the Midlands like in 1912?

Although written in 1945, the play is set in 1912 (two years before the First World War).

The Midlands was a key area during the **Industrial Revolution** of the early nineteenth century. Towns and cities like Birmingham, Wolverhampton, Coventry and Nottingham became centres for industries such as textiles, coal mining and car manufacture.

The growth of factories meant the need for more workers. Many people had moved from small countryside villages to take the low wages on offer and live in cramped, unhygienic accommodation. The increase in low-skilled workers meant that more goods could be produced which, in turn, made the factory owners very rich.

Although conditions were improving, if people fell ill or were made unemployed, there was still no benefits system to help so they would go hungry and become homeless.

Were men and women equal?

Attitudes towards gender were very different and women were considered to be 'the weaker sex'. Girls were brought up with the main aspirations of marriage and children.

Men dominated all aspects of life: home, workplace, church and government. This is often referred to as a patriarchy.

Men and women had specific roles and social expectations, and this actually became stricter the higher you moved up the class system.

Women in wealthy families were not expected to work. Instead, they looked after the home and took on charitable roles. Women in poorer families took unskilled jobs as domestic servants, shop assistants or factory workers. They were paid less than men and couldn't achieve the same level of promotion. Because of this, many women needed a man to support them so were easily seduced and used.

What political movements were important in 1912?

Trade unions had begun to form with the aim of securing better pay and conditions for workers. In 1912, a successful national strike secured a minimum wage for coal miners.

The Suffragettes were campaigning for gender equality, specifically trying to achieve the vote for women. They weren't successful until after the First World War.

The Labour Party was beginning to gain support.

What were the attitudes to morality in 1912?

Morality, having a clear sense of right and wrong, was central to society partly because the Christian church was still a major influence.

The middle classes wanted to appear especially respectable because they aspired to higher status. However, as the Inspector suggests, their morality didn't often lead to them helping other people, just making judgements against them. There were huge double standards, with people appearing righteous and proper while actually behaving badly in secret.

Big towns and cities were full of temptations – such as sex, gambling and alcohol – so men often enjoyed themselves and hid it from their families (especially if they were married!). Sex outside of marriage was disapproved of, especially for a woman. Eric points out to his father that plenty of Arthur's apparently respectable friends get drunk and womanise.

Many women were unaware of this side of life because a respectable woman didn't hang around in bars or walk the streets after dark. Sybil is a good example of this: she doesn't like Sheila knowing slang like 'squiffy' and has no idea about Eric's real behaviour.

Summary

- Industrial areas had lots of poor workers and a few rich businessmen.
- Different groups were campaigning for class and gender equality.
- Despite the strong influence of the Christian Church on society, people (especially men) weren't always as moral as they seemed.

Questions

QUICK TEST
1. Why were people vulnerable if they fell ill or were unemployed?
2. What different areas of life and society did men take charge of?
3. In what ways were women unequal to men?

EXAM PRACTICE
Look at this conversation from Act 3 between Eric and Arthur:

Eric   I wasn't in love with her or anything – but I liked her – she was pretty and a good sport –

Birling [*harshly*] So you had to go to bed with her?

Eric   Well, I'm old enough to be married, aren't I, and I'm not married, and I hate these fat old tarts round the town – the ones I see some of your respectable friends with –

Birling [*angrily*] I don't want any of that talk from you –

Relating your ideas to the historical and social context, write a paragraph explaining how Priestley presents different attitudes to morality in this extract.

The Birlings' House

You must be able to: comment on how the staging of the play reveals things about the characters and themes.

How should stage directions be written about?

Remember that this is a play and don't analyse the specific language of the stage directions. This is because stage directions are there to be performed not spoken aloud.

Instead, think about the effect of the stage directions. How do they affect the mood on stage? What do different things represent or **symbolise**? How do they show what characters are thinking and feeling?

How does J.B. Priestley describe the dining-room set?

The dining-room of a fairly large suburban house, belonging to a prosperous manufacturer. It has good solid furniture of the period. The general effect is substantial and heavily comfortable, but not cosy and homelike. [...]

The lighting should be pink and intimate until the Inspector arrives, and then it should be brighter and harder.

At rise of curtain, the four BIRLINGS and GERALD are seated at the table, with ARTHUR BIRLING at one end, his wife at the other. ERIC downstage, and SHEILA and GERALD seated upstage. EDNA, the parlour-maid, is just clearing the table, which has no cloth, of dessert plates and champagne glasses, etc., and then replacing them with decanter of port, cigar box and cigarettes. Port glasses are already on the table.

How does the setting reflect the family?

The set should show the audience that the Birlings have a high social status. This comes across through the size of the room. This is additionally shown in the expensive furniture, with its sturdiness also **symbolising** how confident the family are in their lives.

It is significant that all five characters are seated, which shows they are currently relaxed. In addition, it underlines their social superiority by contrasting with their maid, Edna, who is on her feet and clearing up after them.

However, the 'suburban' house (which means town or city rather than the countryside) shows the audience that this status is limited. They aren't upper class like the Crofts (which is why Arthur is so desperate for a status-changing knighthood).

Similarly, the general look of the stage shouldn't be warm and comfortable; this implies that there is something missing in this family: love.

How do the props reflect the family?

Different props reflect the family's wealth, in particular the champagne glasses. This is useful to represent the difference between Arthur Birling and Eva Smith: they show the Birlings' wealth but champagne is also a stark contrast to the bleach that Eva drank to kill herself.

How is lighting used on stage?

Priestley is very specific about the lighting, which creates a rosy glow. This symbolises how the Birlings view themselves by making the audience think of the saying, "rose-tinted glasses", about only seeing the best things in life. The Birlings are self-satisfied and ignore the immoral things that they do, partly because they don't see those things as wrong.

The entrance of the Inspector requires the lighting to change, with its increased brightness reflecting how the Birlings' lives are being examined and exposed. This altered lighting should help to create a mood of discomfort on stage.

Key Quotations to Learn

'substantial and heavily comfortable, but not cosy and homelike'

'pink and intimate ... brighter and harder'

'champagne glasses'

Summary

- The dining-room set and its props reflect the Birlings' wealth and self-satisfaction. However, the set also reveals underlying problems in their lives.
- The set creates a visual contrast between the Birlings and the life of Eva Smith.
- The lighting emphasises how the Inspector shines a spotlight on their behaviour.

Questions

QUICK TEST
1. What features of the setting show the Birlings are wealthy?
2. What fault is pointed out about the appearance of the dining-room?
3. How does the set establish that the characters are relaxed and happy?
4. When, how, and why should the lighting alter?

EXAM PRACTICE
Using one or more of the 'Key Quotations to Learn', write a paragraph explaining how the set shows the Birlings' social superiority. Remember to focus on the effect that is created on stage and what this shows the audience.

Inspector Goole

You must be able to: analyse how Inspector Goole is presented in the play.

What does the Inspector represent?

The Inspector is described in his first stage directions as not needing physical size but projecting '[*an impression of massiveness, solidity and purposefulness*]'. This is to highlight that he brings with him symbolic powers of knowledge, morality and judgement.

He embodies the socialist viewpoint that members of society should care about each other. He is also a figure of morality and judgement.

Priestley uses the Inspector to expose one family's **hypocrisy** and their lack of morals and compassion. The change in lighting on stage ('[*brighter and harder*]') symbolises how he has come to reveal their secrets.

How is the Inspector presented as mysterious?

At the end of the play, we find out that there is no such Inspector Goole at the local police station.

However, he is mysterious throughout the play. Like an **omniscient** narrator in a novel, he appears to know everything about the Birlings already. Sheila refers to this at the end of Act 1.

His behaviour also establishes mystery as he doesn't behave quite as the audience expect from a police inspector. He stares at characters before he speaks to them for the first time, refuses to let them see the photograph of Eva Smith until it is their turn and is clearly judgemental rather than **objective**.

Priestley's use of wordplay in Goole/ghoul suggests the character might not be a man but a higher power come to stand in judgement on the Birlings.

How does the Inspector create conflict and tension?

Priestley creates tension through the Inspector by having him ignore social **conventions**. Despite being of a lower class, he has all the power on stage. For example, he is not intimidated by Arthur or Gerald: '[*cutting through massively*]', '[*coolly, looking hard at him*]'.

He doesn't mind upsetting characters or challenging them, such as his effect on Sheila or his questioning of Sybil.

Priestley also uses the Inspector to turn the characters on each other. His presence creates arguments between the parents and their children, as well as ending Sheila and Gerald's engagement.

Key Quotations to Learn

'Yes, but you can't. It's too late. She's dead' (Act 1)

'Apologize for what – doing my duty?' (Act 2)

'their lives, their hopes and fears, their suffering, and chance of happiness' (Act 3)

Summary

- Inspector Goole is a mysterious and powerful figure.
- He is not intimidated by the Birlings' superior class.
- He displays socialism and morality.
- He creates conflict and exposes the other characters on stage.

Sample Analysis

Part of the Inspector's importance is the way in which he challenges Mr and Mrs Birling. Despite the Birlings being of a higher class, the Inspector seems more powerful. This is particularly shown through his use of orders and questioning, 'Don't stammer and yammer at me again, man. *What did she say?*', with Priestley using the Inspector to assert that no-one is above the law. The way the Inspector ignores the social conventions of the time could also suggest his contempt for the family's sense of superiority and that he won't let the Birlings evade their responsibilities.

Questions

QUICK TEST

1. What socialist view does the Inspector represent?
2. How does he seem to go against social conventions?
3. What is unusual about his surname?
4. In what way does he expose the other characters?

EXAM PRACTICE

Using one or more of the 'Key Quotations to Learn', write a paragraph exploring the significance of Inspector Goole in the play.

Arthur Birling

You must be able to: analyse how Arthur Birling is presented in the play.

How is Birling presented as self-satisfied?

At the start of the play, Birling shows off his wealth and experience.

He boasts about the quality of his port and cigars, and praises his own qualities (twice repeating the phrase 'hard-headed business man').

His values of selfishness and survival of the fittest are shown in his words to Eric and Gerald: 'a man has to make his own way – has to look after himself'.

How does Priestley show Birling is the head of the house?

Arthur Birling is a **patriarch**. He is placed symbolically at *'one end'* of the table to show his importance.

He gives orders, such as telling Sybil to praise the cook. Significantly, the cook isn't named (he may not know or care) and he presumably considers it below himself to speak to her personally. This shows his attitude to the working class, as well as to women and their roles.

Birling interrupts other characters and makes long speeches. Priestley gives him the most lines in the opening of the play to demonstrate his dominance.

Because he expects to be respected, he is regularly angered by the way the Inspector interrupts or ignores him.

How are Birling's aspirations revealed?

Birling has gained lots of money but not the social status he wants. His *'provincial'* accent shows he isn't upper class but his hope for a knighthood reveals he wants to be.

His lack of natural class is a personal grievance, acknowledging that Gerald's mother thinks the Birlings are socially **inferior**.

He is happy for Sheila's engagement, partly due to the status it gives him through the Croft name: 'Crofts Limited are both older and bigger than Birling and Company – and now you've brought us together'.

How can the audience tell that Birling isn't as wise as he thinks?

Although written in 1945, the play is set in 1912, which allows Birling to be wrong in his confident speeches about the future.

This is **dramatic irony** and is most obvious in his lines about war ('And I say there isn't a chance of war') and the Titanic ('unsinkable, absolutely unsinkable'). Techniques such as short sentences and repetition are used to emphasise his errors. Priestley also uses the Titanic to **foreshadow** the sinking of the Birlings: the ship's unsinkable luxury mirrors the family's self-assured, wealthy appearance.

Key Quotations to Learn

'working together – for lower costs and higher prices' (Act 1)

'You've a lot to learn yet. And I'm talking as a hard-headed, practical man of business' (Act 1)

'And we don't guess – we've had experience – and we *know*' (Act 1)

Summary

- Arthur Birling is a dominant, patriarchal figure.
- He is wealthy and pleased with himself but wishes for greater social status.
- He believes he has wisdom and experience but Priestley uses dramatic irony to undermine this.

Sample Analysis

Birling is used by Priestley to criticise the role of the **traditional**, early 20th century patriarch. Birling is made to seem dominant in the way he controls conversations, 'Now you three young people, just listen to this – ', and demands the attention of the younger generation. However, as the play progresses we begin to realise that his sense of experience and wisdom is deeply flawed. Priestley is suggesting that young people need new ideas and values, rather than simply maintaining the old order.

Questions

QUICK TEST
1. Why does Priestley give Birling the greatest number of lines and have him interrupt and give orders?
2. What phrase does he repeat to show his self-confidence?
3. As well as his love for his daughter, why is he pleased about her engagement to Gerald?
4. Why is Birling's confident belief that there will be no war important?

EXAM PRACTICE
Using one or more of the 'Key Quotations to Learn', write a paragraph exploring the significance of Arthur Birling in the play.

You must be able to: analyse how Mrs Birling is presented in the play.

What kind of woman is Sybil?

Sybil is presented as a traditional early-twentieth century middle class woman, focussed on the household and her children. Although she is his social superior, and sometimes tells him off for a lack of correct **etiquette**, she usually defers to her husband and follows his lead. She is told to pass on a message to the cook, accepts that men 'spend nearly all their time and energy on their business', leaves the room with Sheila so the men can talk together and looks to Arthur to take charge.

How is Sybil presented as feeling superior?

When she meets the Inspector, she thinks she is above him and speaks '[*haughtily*]' and '[*rather grandly*]'. She is surprised by his lack of respect, 'That – I consider – is a trifle impertinent, Inspector'.

To assert herself, she refers to her husband's social position.

She suggests she is better than other characters, taking a moralistic view of Gerald's affair when calling it 'disgusting' and, in Act 3, boasting that she was the 'only one of you who didn't give in' to the Inspector.

How does Priestley show her hypocrisy?

Sybil presents herself as moralistic, with a prominent role in the Brumley Women's Charity Organisation. She talks about helping others and doing her duty.

However, she turned down Eva's application for support, looking down on her for being single and pregnant. She refers to 'that sort' of girl, showing her dislike of the lower classes and what she sees as Eva's lack of sexual decency.

Throughout the play, she refuses to accept any blame and excuses herself by repeating the word **'justified'**.

She criticises Eva's lover's lack of morals but these turn out to be the qualities of her own son.

How is Sybil presented as a bad mother?

Sybil does not really know her children, particularly Eric. She doesn't realise he has a drinking problem and cannot believe he could ever have an affair. He subsequently accuses her of having killed her own grandchild and tells her she never tried to understand him.

Mr Birling calls Eric 'spoiled' and this reflects on Sybil's parenting skills.

She also belittles her children, not wanting them to grow up or develop their own views: 'He's only a boy', 'It would be much better if Sheila didn't listen to this story at all'.

Key Quotations to Learn

'Girls of that class – ' (Act 2)

'I think she only had herself to blame' (Act 2)

'Besides, you're not that type – you don't get drunk – ' (Act 3)

Summary

- Mrs Birling displays a traditional female role in the house.
- She sees herself as superior to people of the lower classes.
- She presents herself as moral and charitable.
- She is revealed to be a hypocrite and a bad mother.

Sample Analysis

Priestley uses the character of Sybil to explore what he saw as a lack of social responsibility amongst the middle classes at the time. This is shown throughout the play by her refusal to accept any blame for what happened to Eva Smith, 'So I was perfectly justified in advising my committee not to allow her claim', displaying her stubborn and selfish attitude as she excuses her actions. Priestley encourages the audience to judge Sybil's lack of compassion through the way he has her show off her social power and the fact that she could have helped Eva if she had wanted to.

Questions

QUICK TEST
1. In what ways does Sybil conform to the gender expectations of the time?
2. Why does she feel superior to others?
3. What does her charity role show about her?
4. What is her relationship with Eric like?

EXAM PRACTICE
Using one or more of the 'Key Quotations to Learn', write a paragraph exploring the significance of Sybil Birling in the play.

Sheila Birling

You must be able to: analyse how Sheila is presented in the play.

What is Sheila's life like?

The opening stage direction says that Sheila should be presented as '[*very pleased with life and rather excited*]'.

She is in her 20s and has an easy life. Following the traditional social expectations for a daughter of a wealthy family in the early twentieth century, Sheila doesn't work. She is obedient to her parents and engaged to marry Gerald.

She still refers to her parents as 'Mummy' and 'Daddy', suggesting her class and also her childishness.

What does her treatment of Eva Smith show about her?

She has Eva sacked because she felt she was mocking her. Sheila admits she over-reacted because she was in a bad mood and was jealous that the girl was prettier than her.

She uses her social power, as a good customer who is about to marry a wealthy man, to have a lower-class girl punished.

How does Sheila respond to her actions?

When she first hears of Eva Smith's death, she is sympathetic but more focussed on how it's made her sad, 'I've been so happy tonight. Oh I wish you hadn't told me'.

This self-centred response continues when she realises she had Eva sacked from Milwards, 'I feel now I can never go there again'.

These responses reflect the selfish values that she has been brought up with.

However, in Act 2, she begins to reflect more on her responsibility: 'And I know I'm to blame – and I'm desperately sorry – but I can't believe – I won't believe – it's simply my fault that in the end she – committed suicide'. Her guilt is still **juxtaposed** with a refusal to take ultimate responsibility but the use of dashes indicates that her speech should sound uncertain, as if struggling with her **conscience**.

How is Sheila presented as more insightful than her family?

Whereas Arthur, Sybil, and Gerald deny their responsibility and try to cover up their involvement, Sheila quickly realises that they cannot hide the truth.

At the end of Act 2, she contributes to the increasing tension by trying to stop her mother from incriminating herself and Eric (having already worked out that he fathered Eva's child).

Key Quotations to Learn

'I'll never, never do it again to anybody' (Act 1)

'No, he's giving us rope – so that we'll hang ourselves' (Act 2)

'Mother – I begged you and begged you to stop' (Act 2)

Summary

- Sheila has an easy happy life and a high social status.
- She used her status to have Eva sacked.
- She shows some guilt for what happened but is also busy feeling sorry for herself.
- Unlike the rest of the family, she realises that the Inspector already knows the full story.

Sample Analysis

Sheila is used many times by Priestley to create tension on stage. She realises the family's position long before the others, '[*urgently, cutting in*] Mother, don't – please don't. For your own sake, as well as ours', and tries to warn her mother. As well as the sense of danger, Priestley is creating conflict because, at the time, the younger generation weren't expected to interrupt their parents or claim greater wisdom. In addition, Priestley maintains the audience's disapproval of the Birlings as, despite feeling some guilt about Eva, Sheila is still clearly focussed on her own well-being.

Questions

QUICK TEST
1. Why does Sheila have social status?
2. What feelings cause her to have Eva sacked?
3. How does Sheila begin to change?
4. What does she realise about Eric, long before the rest of the family?

EXAM PRACTICE
Using one or more of the 'Key Quotations to Learn', write a paragraph exploring the significance of Sheila Birling in the play.

Eric Birling

You must be able to: analyse how Eric is presented in the play.

What first impressions are the audience given of Eric?

At the start of the play, Eric seems an outsider. He is the last character to speak and is absent from the second act.

The opening stage direction describes him as '[*not quite at ease*]' and this appears throughout Act 1, such as when he stops himself mid-sentence during a discussion about women and his reaction to Gerald's joke about misbehaviour.

He first gains the audience's attention when he bursts out laughing for no reason. This, and his squabble with Sheila, makes him seem immature. Mr and Mrs Birling regularly talk down to him, for example, 'Silly boy!', despite him being in his 20s.

Priestley draws attention to his drinking through the stage directions and this becomes more important later on.

How does he feel about what he has done?

Unlike the others, Eric makes no attempt to excuse his behaviour.

The stage directions repeatedly point out that he should speak '[*miserably*]'. He is clearly ashamed of his actions and this helps to explain his strange and distant behaviour at the start of the play.

How does Eric clash with his parents?

Early on, he displays different values to his father. He suggests that Eva was right to go on strike and receives an angry response from Arthur.

When Eric returns in Act 3, the family have been discussing his behaviour and, especially Sybil, making the situation worse for him. Instead of supporting him, his parents are angry about the impending scandal. When he asks for a drink, his father refuses '[*explosively*]' but the Inspector agrees, saying 'look at him. He needs a drink now just to see him through'.

He later tells his father that he's never been able to talk to him and he says a similar thing to his mother: 'You don't understand anything. You never did. You never even tried – you – '.

When he finds out that his mother turned Eva away from the charity, he accuses her of killing her own grandchild.

After the Inspector has left, Mr Birling singles Eric out as the person to blame.

Key Quotations to Learn

'Why shouldn't they try for higher wages?' (Act 1)

'I hate these fat old tarts round the town – the ones I see some of your respectable friends with – ' (Act 3)

'you killed them both – damn you, damn you – ' (Act 3)

Sample Analysis

Priestley uses Eric to explore the theme of shame. When he describes his first night with Eva, 'And I didn't even remember – that's the hellish thing. Oh – my God! – how stupid it all is!', Eric seems genuinely distressed and repentant. The use of religious language could link to the significance of Christianity in society at the time, suggesting that he sees himself as sinful and is confessing to the Inspector. Although Priestley is criticising male attitudes towards lower class women, he is also using Eric's shame to contrast with the lack of regret shown by Mr and Mrs Birling.

Summary

- Eric acts strangely at the start of the play.
- His behaviour is explained when it is revealed that he made Eva pregnant.
- The play gradually builds up the fact that he has a drink problem.
- He clashes with his parents and this reaches a climax just before the Inspector leaves.

Questions

QUICK TEST
1. Why does Eric seem different to the other characters at the start of the play?
2. How does he disagree with his father about the factory workers?
3. How does he feel about his behaviour?
4. What does he feel about his relationship with his parents?

EXAM PRACTICE
Using one or more of the 'Key Quotations to Learn', write a paragraph exploring the significance of Eric Birling in the play.

Gerald Croft

You must be able to: analyse how Gerald is presented in the play.

What is Gerald's relationship with Arthur like?

Gerald has a fairly equal relationship with Arthur. This is mainly because he is of a higher class, being the son of Sir George and Lady Croft, so Arthur respects him and hopes to gain status through him.

Like Arthur, Gerald is a businessman. When Eric argues with his father about the factory strike, Gerald sides with Arthur's viewpoint: 'I should say so!'

Although Birling lectures Gerald, he also confides in him about the possibility of his knighthood. It is clear that Mr and Mrs Birling like and trust their future son-in-law.

How does Priestley present Gerald's relationship with Eva Smith?

Gerald knew Eva as Daisy Renton. He initially denies it but Sheila sees through his lies. He plans to keep it a secret from the Inspector but Sheila says he won't be able to.

When he met Daisy, he found her attractive and felt sorry for her so he gave her money and a place to stay. He just wanted to help her but she became his mistress as well: 'I suppose it was inevitable. She was young and pretty and warm-hearted – and intensely grateful'. The dash creates a pause to suggest Gerald realises that Eva may have felt obliged because he was her only support.

He admits that she loved him more than he loved her and he eventually broke off the relationship. He is distressed when he thinks about her death.

How do the other characters' opinions of him change?

In contrast to their happiness at the start, once Sheila works out about the affair she loses respect for Gerald: 'Oh don't be stupid. We haven't much time'. As he tells his story, she mocks him, 'You were the wonderful Fairy Prince. You must have adored it, Gerald'.

After his confession, Sheila says she believes his intentions were initially good but she can no longer be his fiancée: 'You and I aren't the same people who sat down to dinner here'.

Sybil calls his story a, 'disgusting affair', which contrasts with the start of the play when she stops Sheila from teasing Gerald for having worked so much over the summer (when he was actually with Daisy).

Perhaps for selfish reasons, Arthur doesn't particularly change his opinion of Gerald. When Sheila breaks off the engagement, he tries to reason with her, 'Now, Sheila, I'm not defending him. But you must understand that a lot of young men – '.

Key Quotations to Learn

'we're respectable citizens and not criminals' (Act 1)

'We can keep it from him' (Act 1)

'She didn't blame me at all. I wish to God she had now' (Act 2)

Summary

- The Birlings are happy to have Gerald as Sheila's fiancé.
- He tries to hide his relationship with Eva/Daisy from Sheila and the Inspector.
- Gerald wanted to help Eva/Daisy but it turned into an affair.
- He is upset by the news of Eva's death and understands when Sheila breaks off the engagement.

Sample Analysis

Gerald's temporary regret is an important feature of the play as Priestley uses it to explore middle class selfishness. Gerald is clearly upset by Eva Smith's death, '[*distressed*] Sorry – I – well, I've suddenly realised – taken it in properly – that she's dead –', and appears to recognise the consequences of his actions. However, by the end of the play, when he believes the evening has been a hoax, it is clear that he was concerned about the consequences to his own life rather than that of Eva. This suggests that the class issues Priestley is highlighting are deep-rooted and difficult to change.

Questions

QUICK TEST
1. In what ways does Gerald pretend to be something that he's not?
2. Why does Arthur like Gerald?
3. What were the honourable aspects of his part in Eva Smith's life?
4. What were the dishonourable aspects of his part in Eva Smith's life?

EXAM PRACTICE
Using one or more of the 'Key Quotations to Learn', write a paragraph exploring the significance of Gerald Croft in the play.

You must be able to: analyse how Eva Smith and Edna are presented in the play.

How does Priestley present Eva Smith?

Eva Smith never appears on stage; instead, the audience are given details about her by the other characters. This is important because it symbolises how the working classes play a large role in the Birlings' life and wealth but they are almost invisible.

The Inspector explains that she has committed suicide by drinking disinfectant. He later reveals that she was pregnant.

Arthur describes her as a lively, hard-working girl. Like Gerald and Sheila, he also comments on her good looks.

She is presented as moral (she won't take Eric's stolen money) and having a strong belief in fairness and equality (organising the strike at the factory). It is significant that she comes across as having better values than the people who ruined her life.

Eva also used the name Daisy Renton.

What is Eva Smith being used to represent?

Eva is used by Priestley as an 'every-woman' and he draws attention to this by giving her the common surname 'Smith'.

She represents the working classes: both their financial struggles and the prejudice against them from those of a higher status.

She also shows the audience some of the obstacles that women faced in society:

- The **dominance** of men (Arthur is her employer, Eric forces his way into her lodgings).
- Being treated like a sexual object (Joe Meggarty's advances, Eric only wanting her for sex).
- The difficulty in being independent or self-sufficient (she is unemployed and hungry when she meets Gerald and she is dependent on his support).
- Prejudice about sexual activity (Sybil is prejudiced against her partly because she is pregnant but unmarried).

What is the significance of Edna?

Although she is not on stage a great deal, Edna is another representation of the working classes. She is a servant, cleaning away the table and fetching drinks.

The Birlings mostly ignore her but Arthur and Sybil acknowledge her presence in relation to the jobs they want doing.

She is addressed informally as 'Edna' but she responds to her employers as 'ma'am' or 'sir', showing the differences in status between the classes.

Key Quotations to Learn

Inspector: 'There are a lot of young women living that sort of existence in every city and big town in this country' (Act 1)

Inspector: 'She was here alone, friendless, almost penniless, desperate'
(Act 2)

Inspector: 'Just used her [...] as if she was an animal, a thing, not a person' (Act 3)

Summary

- Eva is only described by others, never seen.
- She has committed suicide.
- She represents the plight of working class women.
- She is shown to have better values than the seemingly more respectable Birlings.

Eva Smith's Timeline

Sep 1910	After helping to organise a strike over wages at Birling and Company, Eva is sacked.
Dec 1910	She gets a job at Milwards.
Jan 1911	Sheila complains about Eva and she is sacked.
March 1911	Eva, who has now changed her name to Daisy Renton, meets Gerald. He finds her a place to live and she becomes his lover.
Sep 1911	Gerald breaks off his relationship with Daisy. She goes to live by the seaside for two months.
Nov 1911	Eva meets Eric. They become lovers and she gets pregnant. After she realises that Eric is supporting her with stolen money, she leaves him.
Spring 1912	Eva, using the name Mrs Birling, asks for help from the Brumley Women's Charity Organisation but it is refused.
Spring 1912	Two weeks later, Eva Smith commits suicide.

Questions

QUICK TEST
1. Which two sections of society does Eva Smith represent?
2. In what different ways is she treated badly by characters in the play?
3. In what ways does she appear to have better values than the Birlings?
4. What does Edna show about the Birlings' attitude to the working class?

EXAM PRACTICE
Using one or more of the 'Key Quotations to Learn', write a paragraph exploring the importance of the working class in the play.

How the Characters Change

You must be able to: analyse how the characters change during the play.

Arthur and Sybil Birling

Mr and Mrs Birling change the least in the play. Their treatment of Eva Smith is exposed and their relationship with their children is damaged. The audience see their confidence and status weakened. However, once the Inspector leaves and they decide it was all a hoax, they go back to their old, self-centred ways. Arthur even makes a joke about the evening: '[Imitating Inspector in his final speech] *You all helped to kill her.* [Pointing at Sheila and Eric, and laughing]'.

Gerald

Like Arthur and Sybil, once Gerald decides it is a hoax, he cheers up and tries to get Sheila to wear the engagement ring again. The audience are shown his disregard for the working classes when he says, 'What girl? There were probably four or five different girls'. He does not mind how many girls' lives have been ruined so long as it isn't going to be a public scandal.

Sheila and Eric

The Birling children are most affected by the events of the play. Priestley does this to reflect society's changing values between the young and the old, suggesting that the young represent hope for a more equal, compassionate future.

Sheila's distress and regret can be seen as early as Act 1 but it is often focussed on her feeling sorry for herself.

By the end of the play, Sheila feels genuine remorse and she realises that it doesn't matter if the Inspector was real or not, 'I tell you – whoever that Inspector was, it was anything but a joke'.

She wants her family to change their ways and Priestley has her repeat the Inspector's words, 'Fire and blood and anguish', to show that she understands his revolutionary warning.

Eric is similarly altered and describes himself as frightened by the Inspector's final words.

Priestley focuses on Eric's broken relationship with his parents: '[*quietly, bitterly*] I don't give a damn now whether I stay here or not'.

Key Quotations to Learn

Arthur: 'there'll be a public scandal – unless we're lucky – and who here will suffer from that more than I will?'

Sheila: 'you don't seem to have learnt anything' (Act 3)

Eric: 'You're beginning to pretend now that nothing's really happened'

Mrs Birling: 'In the morning they'll be as amused as we are'

Gerald: 'Everything's alright now, Sheila'

Summary

- Arthur, Sybil and Gerald do not really change. Although disturbed by the night's events, once they decide it's a hoax, they return to normal.
- Sheila and Eric are upset and regret their actions. They can't understand their parents' attitudes and begin to see they must all change their behaviour.

Sample Analysis

Priestley uses the lack of change in Mr Birling's character to assert the need for social change, criticising class prejudice and selfish social attitudes. In Act 1, Mr Birling believes that the working classes need to be kept in their place, 'If you don't come down sharply on some of these people', showing that he sees the workers as all the same rather than individuals to be cared for. This outlook is still held at the end of the play, 'Probably a Socialist or some sort of crank', with ideas of equality and compassion being ridiculed. Priestley promotes the virtues of socialism by having it disparaged by a character whose lack of values has been exposed to the audience.

Questions

QUICK TEST
1. What is Arthur most worried about once the Inspector has left?
2. In what way do Eric and Sheila's attitudes at the end of the play differ to those of their parents?
3. What does Gerald ask Sheila that shows he thinks nothing has changed?
4. What has changed between Eric and his parents?

EXAM PRACTICE
Using one of the 'Key Quotations to Learn', write a paragraph exploring the importance of change in the play.

Morality

You must be able to: analyse how the theme of morality is presented in the play.

What is morality?

Morality is a sense of right and wrong. It is often linked to religion but Priestley explores it in terms of society, considering personal behaviour and the treatment of others.

Which characters see themselves as 'moral'?

Gerald and the Birlings base their sense of morality on their class. Because they have status they assume they are superior. Priestley challenges this view in Act 1:

Gerald: We're respectful citizens and not criminals.

Inspector: Sometimes there isn't as much difference as you think.

Sybil presumes moral superiority when she feels her charity work gives her the right to judge others. When she is called a 'prominent' member of the charity, Priestley is suggesting the role is more about making herself look good in society.

How does Priestley use the seven deadly sins?

Priestley draws on Christian ideas to shows his characters' lack of social morality.

When the play begins, the audience see the sin of *gluttony* (eating and drinking wastefully or to excess). The table is being cleared of '[*dessert plates and champagne glasses, etc.*]' and everyone is drinking port. Priestley uses this scene to contrast, in Act 2, with Gerald describing Eva as being hungry. Eric, through his drinking, becomes the particular focus of this sin.

Arthur is guilty of *greed* through his desire for more money and status. When he describes his 'duty to keep labour costs down', Priestley uses the **noun** 'duty' ironically to show Birling's lack of moral understanding.

He is also full of *wrath* or anger throughout the play, sacking Eva partly out of anger and losing his temper with the Inspector and his children.

Sheila represents *envy*, for having Eva sacked partly out of jealousy over her prettiness. This links to wrath, as she admits to being in a bad mood, while her lifestyle suggests *sloth* or laziness. Sloth also relates to the other characters' social laziness as they are unwilling to support people in need.

Sybil's *pride* is obvious in the way she speaks, regularly emphasising her status, such as the stress on the personal pronoun in the line, '*I'm* talking to the Inspector now'.

Gerald and Eric display *lust* when each makes Eva their mistress and loves her less than she loves them. This sin is extended to Joe Meggarty and Arthur's friends to criticise their attitudes to women.

Key Quotations to Learn

Inspector: 'you might be said to have been jealous of her' (Act 1)

Sybil: 'she called herself Mrs Birling [...] a piece of gross impertinence' (Act 2)

Eric: 'I wasn't in love with her or anything' (Act 3)

Summary

- The characters consider themselves to be moral because of their social status.
- They lack social morality and compassion for the people around them.
- Priestley links the Birlings and Gerald to the seven deadly sins.

Sample Analysis

Priestley presents a lack of morality amongst Brumley's middle classes in order to expose the hypocrisy he saw in society's class prejudices. When Gerald reveals that a town councillor, Joe Meggarty, is 'a notorious womanizer as well as being one of the worst sots and rogues', Priestley links him to the Christian sins of lust and gluttony. By making it clear that people know about Meggarty's behaviour and yet he still holds a position of responsibility, Priestley criticises the higher classes' abuse of power and how they ignore in themselves what they condemn in people of lower status.

Questions

QUICK TEST
1. How is Arthur linked to the sin of greed?
2. How is Eric linked to lust and gluttony?
3. What was Sheila envious of?
4. Where is Sybil shown to consider herself as morally superior to others?

EXAM PRACTICE
Using one or more of the 'Key Quotations to Learn', write a paragraph exploring the importance of morality in the play.

Survival of the Fittest

You must be able to: analyse how the theme of survival is presented in the play.

What is survival of the fittest?

This term was first used in the late 1800s to describe how, in the animal kingdom, weak species die out and the strongest survive. In a capitalist society, people with power and money will usually do better than those without. The term is sometimes used by capitalists to justify selfish economic behaviour (such as very low wages or trying to put others out of business).

What is Arthur's view?

Arthur promotes the idea of survival of the fittest to Eric and Gerald, telling them that a man 'has to look after himself [...] so long as he does that he won't come to much harm'.

His words are selfish and, near the end of the play, Eric mocks how these words returned to haunt his father: '[*laughs bitterly*] I didn't notice you told him that it's every man for himself'.

What does the Inspector think?

It is symbolic that, when he gives his selfish speech to Eric and Gerald, Arthur is interrupted by the Inspector's arrival: '[*We hear the sharp ring of a front door bell. Birling stops to listen*]'.

Part of the Inspector's role is to challenge Arthur's view of the survival of the fittest. He can be seen as representing Priestley's socialist views.

When Arthur explains his refusal to pay his workers more, the Inspector says 'Why?' This simple question implies how unfair Arthur has been. Their clash of viewpoints is seen in Arthur's response: '[*surprised*] Did you say "why?"?' His tone of voice and the repetition of the Inspector's question show that, to Arthur, placing one's own interests above those of others is the normal way to behave.

The Inspector suggests a different, more compassionate life based on empathy, 'it would do us all a bit of good if sometimes we tried to put ourselves in the place of these young women counting their pennies in their dingy little back bedrooms'.

How does this link to Eva Smith?

Eva represents the consequences of the survival of the fittest attitude.

Blaming the Birlings for putting their own lives above that of Eva, the Inspector describes her dead body as, 'A nice little promising life there, I thought, and a nasty mess someone's made of it'.

Key Quotations to Learn

Arthur: 'a man has to make his own way' (Act 1)

Inspector (about Eva): 'But she died in misery and agony – hating life' (Act 2)

Inspector: 'all intertwined with our lives, with what we think and say and do' (Act 3)

Summary

- Arthur believes in survival of the fittest: looking after your own interests at the expense of others.
- The Inspector provides the opposite view that members of society should look after each other.
- Eva Smith is used to represent the consequence of Arthur's viewpoint.

Sample Analysis

Priestley uses Mr Birling's belief in the survival of the fittest to offer a criticism of the social values of the time. When Eric and Gerald are advised that, 'a man has to mind his own business', the audience sees Mr Birling's belief in the importance of making money and ignoring the plight of others. He emphasises the need to, 'look after himself and his own', promoting selfishness as well as the idea that poorer people are somehow different or below him. This refusal to see himself as part of a wider society contrasts with Priestley's own socialist values and is eventually Mr Birling's downfall.

Questions

QUICK TEST
1. Who does Arthur encourage to follow self-interest?
2. What is symbolic about the arrival of the Inspector?
3. How does Eva represent the consequences of self-interest?
4. How are Arthur's words about self-interest reused by Eric in Act 3?

EXAM PRACTICE
Using one or more of the 'Key Quotations to Learn', write a paragraph exploring the importance of compassion in the play.

Social Responsibility

You must be able to: analyse how social responsibility is explored in the play.

What is social responsibility?

Priestley uses the play to express his belief that we should help those people in society who are less fortunate than us. This is a key principle of socialism. He believes that capitalism focuses too much on individual gain.

How does Arthur Birling present social responsibility?

Arthur doesn't believe in social responsibility. His views are based on his capitalist ideals. He feels a responsibility to his family and his business, not to other people: 'it's my duty to keep labour costs down'.

He believes the poor are greedy and that the rich need to be careful, not caring, about them: 'they'd soon be asking for the earth'.

For him to be wealthy and happy, he thinks others must naturally be poor and unhappy.

How does Sybil Birling present social responsibility?

Despite being a prominent member of the Brumley Women's Charity Organisation, Sybil also lacks social responsibility. They help girls who are 'deserving cases', suggesting the organisation is judgemental rather than compassionate.

She doesn't like Eva Smith and makes sure her case is refused. It is implied that she doesn't want to help because Eva is an unmarried mother, linking to the moral values of the time.

She refers to Eva as 'a girl of that sort' who was giving herself 'ridiculous airs'. This shows that she thinks working class girls are below her and should know their place.

How does the Inspector present social responsibility?

The Inspector is used by Priestley to promote social responsibility, 'their lives, their hopes and fears, their suffering, and chance of happiness, all intertwined with our lives, with what we think and say and do'.

The Inspector focuses on the vulnerable in society and how they need help: 'She needed not only money, but advice, sympathy, friendliness'.

When talking to Gerald and Sheila, he highlights his belief in social responsibility by including himself in the blame for Eva Smith's death, 'we'll have to share our guilt'.

He wants the Birlings to change, 'Remember what you did, Mrs Birling'.

Although the older members of the family don't seem to change, Sheila and Eric's outlook is altered by the Inspector.

Key Quotations to Learn

Arthur: 'like bees in a hive – community and all that nonsense' (Act 1)

Inspector: 'it would do us all a bit of good if sometimes we tried to put ourselves in the place of these young women' (Act 1)

Inspector: 'You must have known what she was feeling. And you slammed the door in her face' (Act 2)

Summary

- Priestley uses the Inspector to express the importance of social responsibility.
- He uses Arthur and Sybil Birling to represent how the higher classes focus on improving their own lives and status, rather than helping others.
- The Inspector changes Sybil and Eric's social viewpoint but Arthur, Sybil and Gerald quickly return to their old selfishness.

Sample Analysis

The importance of social responsibility is presented through the character of the Inspector. He becomes a mouthpiece for Priestley's socialist values, especially towards the end of the play. His comments about society, 'We don't live alone. We are members of one body. We are responsible for each other', emphasise socialist values of joint responsibility. The message that we should all respect and help each other seems shaped by the events of the first and second world wars when the country had to pull together and overcome individual differences.

Questions

QUICK TEST
1. What does the Inspector believe we should do for the less fortunate people in society?
2. What is Arthur's opinion of social responsibility?
3. In what way does Sybil only pretend to have social responsibility?

EXAM PRACTICE
Using one or more of the 'Key Quotations to Learn', write a paragraph exploring the importance of social responsibility in the play.

Personal Responsibility

You must be able to: analyse how Priestley shows the different characters' attitudes to personal responsibility.

What is personal responsibility?

This means accepting the consequences of your own actions. As well as wanting the Birlings to understand why they should behave differently towards other people, the Inspector challenges each character to admit, and show guilt for, their individual role in Eva's suicide. In Act 3, Sheila refers to this as being made to 'confess'.

This is highlighted in one of the Inspector's final speeches: 'This girl killed herself – and died a horrible death. But each of you helped to kill her. Remember that. Never forget it'. The **emotive** language emphasises the effects of the characters' behaviour, while the two short imperative sentences focus on the necessity of accepting guilt.

Who accepts responsibility?

Sheila and Eric accept that they wronged Eva Smith.

In Act 3, Sheila says, 'I behaved badly too. I know I did. I'm ashamed of it'. Priestley emphasises her guilt through the repetition of the personal pronoun 'I' and uses short sentences that add a tone of certainty about her guilt.

The two children also point out the responsibility of the rest of the family, with Eric stating: 'the fact remains that I did what I did. And Mother did what she did. And the rest of you did what you did to her'. The use of **parallelism** at the end of each sentence emphasises the personal responsibility of everyone in the room, with the repetition of 'and' building up a sense of their negative impact on Eva's life.

Who doesn't accept responsibility?

While Gerald feels guilty in Act 2 for cheating on Sheila and for eventually deserting Eva, by the end of the play – because he thinks no one else knows – he seems to have forgotten his shame. He asks Sheila to remain engaged to him and doubts the story of Eva's death.

Throughout the play, Arthur claims that he was right to sack Eva Smith and justifies it using the word 'duty'. Sybil takes a similar point of view about refusing to help Eva, saying 'I had done no more than my duty'.

Priestley highlights Arthur and Sybil's lack of personal responsibility by also having them point out the failings of others. This is most obvious in the way Sybil, not realising she is criticising Eric, focuses on the responsibility of the man who made Eva pregnant, saying he should be made an example of and be forced to make a public confession.

Key Quotations to Learn

Inspector: 'Remember' (Act 3)

Sybil: 'He certainly didn't make me *confess* – as you call it' (Act 3)

Eric: 'It's what happened to the girl and what we all did to her that matters' (Act 3)

Summary

- The Inspector encourages each character to confess and take personal responsibility for the death of Eva Smith.
- Sheila and Eric accept responsibility.
- Gerald seems to show remorse but this fades when he thinks the story can be kept secret.
- Arthur and Sybil refuse to accept that they did anything wrong.

Sample Analysis

Priestley asserts the importance of personal responsibility by encouraging the audience to deplore Mr Birling's refusal to take any blame for Eva Smith's death. When he says, 'There's every excuse for what both your mother and I did – it turned out unfortunately, that's all', his apparent dismissal of her death shows he has no genuine sympathy. Despite the audience having heard the terrible consequences of his actions, the character attempts to justify what he has done and the additional way that he includes Sybil in the acknowledgment of his involvement shows his reluctance to accept any individual guilt.

Questions

QUICK TEST
1. Which characters take responsibility for their actions?
2. What word does Sheila use to describe the process of admitting what they did?
3. What do Arthur and Sybil do instead of taking responsibility?

EXAM PRACTICE
Using one or more of the 'Key Quotations to Learn', write a paragraph exploring the importance of personal responsibility in the play.

Inequality

You must be able to: analyse how Priestley shows the idea of inequality.

What is inequality?

Priestley's key socialist message is a response to the lack of equality in society. In the play, he explores how a lack of equality makes Eva Smith's life difficult and contributes to her death. Because the Birlings and Gerald have more money, status and power, their lives are much easier.

How does Eva represent inequality?

In terms of social **hierarchies**, Eva is at the bottom because she is working class and a woman. She always has people above her, controlling her life.

This can be seen in her working life, where she was easily fired from the factory and Milwards. It can also be seen in her personal life, forming relationships with Gerald and Eric where she is dependent on them financially and emotionally.

Because of her low status, Eva has a lack of opportunities. When Arthur asks what she did after being sacked, 'Get into trouble? Go on the streets?', crime and prostitution are presented as her most obvious options.

Her life is a struggle and references are made to her being penniless, hungry, lonely and preyed upon – sexually – by more powerful men.

How do the Birlings represent inequality?

In contrast to Eva, the Birlings represent power and fortune. They benefit from inequality.

The dining-room set and the meal they have just finished suggest wealth and an easy lifestyle.

Birling refers to their better opportunities when he mentions Eric's 'public-school-and Varsity life'.

Their power comes from money but also their roles in society: Arthur is a magistrate, has been Lord Mayor, and is expecting a knighthood. In comparison, Eva would not even have had the vote (women didn't have the same voting rights as men until 1928).

As a wealthy client, Sheila has the power to have people sacked from Milwards. Similarly, Sybil has the power to influence who is helped by her charity.

How does the Inspector criticise inequality?

The Inspector criticises how working class girls are seen as 'cheap labour'.

As he investigates the family, he reveals the different ways they made Eva a victim of their social superiority.

He blames inequality for her suicide, saying her reason was 'Because she had been turned out and turned down too many times'. Priestley's use of the **passive voice** and repetition emphasise how Eva wasn't in control of her own life.

Key Quotations to Learn

Arthur: 'we're in for a time of steadily increasing prosperity' (Act 1)

Sheila: 'these girls aren't cheap labour – they're *people*' (Act 1)

Gerald: 'she was desperately hard up' (Act 2)

Summary

- Eva Smith suffers from social inequality due to her class and her gender. There are always more powerful people controlling her life.
- Arthur and his family benefit from inequality as cheap labour has made them rich. Their abuse of power has led to Eva's death.

Sample Analysis

Priestley highlights the effects of inequality through the depiction of Eva's life after she is sacked by Mr Birling. The Inspector's description of her having, 'no work, no money coming in, [...] no relatives to help her, few friends, lonely, half-starved, she was feeling desperate', builds up a sense of Eva's physical, emotional, and economic struggle. Importantly, Priestley uses Eva to represent all the victims of social inequality, making the play as relevant today as it was in the 1940s. Because Priestley places this speech soon after the Birlings' family celebration, the references to hunger and a lack of money and relatives also creates a stark contrast between Eva and the people who have ruined her life.

Questions

QUICK TEST
1. Why is Eva socially unequal?
2. What things suggest the Birlings have greater power and opportunities?
3. How do the Birlings benefit from social inequality?

EXAM PRACTICE
Using one or more of the 'Key Quotations to Learn', write a paragraph exploring the importance of inequality in the play.

Young and Old

You must be able to: analyse how Priestley explores the differences between youth and age.

How are traditional ideas about age shown in the play?

Traditionally, young people are expected to respect and obey their elders.
These expectations were even more rigid at the start of the twentieth century.

When the play begins, Priestley gives Arthur the greatest number of lines to show he is in charge. He toasts the engagement, gives his opinions about the state of the world and goes on to lecture Eric and Gerald about life.

When he talks, he expects people to pay attention ('Are you listening, Sheila?'), doesn't like to be interrupted ('Just let me finish Eric') and gives opinions as facts ('The world's developing so fast it'll make war impossible').

Mrs Birling, although she lets her husband take the lead, also shows this dominance over the young, 'Please don't contradict me like that'.

Before the Inspector arrives, Eric and Sheila behave as tradition demands, for example, stopping squabbling when Sybil tells them off. Even when Eric tells his father not to make a speech, it is said '[*not too rudely*]' so the atmosphere on stage follows normal expectations.

Where are traditional age roles challenged?

When the Inspector arrives, Eric and Sheila begin to challenge the values of their parents. Both criticise Arthur's decision to sack Eva and, in Act 2, Sybil disapprovingly notes, 'You seem to have made a great impression on this child, Inspector'.

Sheila continues to challenge their behaviour, such as telling her father not to 'interfere' when he suggests she forgives Gerald or calling her mother's actions 'cruel and vile'. It is clear that she understands what the Inspector is doing whereas her parents do not.

Eric's response is more extreme. He curses his mother ('damn you'), is aggressive towards her ('[*almost threatening her*]') and mocks the **irony** of Arthur's after-dinner speech about self-interest.

How is Priestley using ideas about age?

By the end of the play, Eric and Sheila offer future hope. They represent the idea that society can change because they challenge their parents' refusal to alter their behaviour, with Sheila saying, 'You're ready to go on in the same old way. [...] And it frightens me the way you talk'.

The Inspector's words have had a positive effect on them and they are beginning to develop a social conscience.

Key Quotations to Learn

Arthur: 'But you youngsters just remember what I said' (Act 1)

Sheila (to Arthur): 'Oh – sorry. I didn't know. Mummy sent me in to ask you' (Act 1)

Eric: '[*shouting*] And I say the girl's dead and we all helped to kill her – and that's what matters – ' (Act 3)

Summary

- The young are expected to respect and obey their elders.
- At first, the Birlings display traditional expectations of age.
- After the Inspector's arrival, Sheila and Eric begin to challenge their parents.
- The children represent hope. Unlike their parents, they can learn and change.

Sample Analysis

Priestley explores the conflict between youth and age through Mr Birling and his son, Eric. In response to having his authority challenged, Mr Birling says, 'So hold your tongue if you want to stay here' to show his anger that the traditional expectations of respect for one's elders are being ignored. The play looks back to a time before the social changes of the 1940s and Priestley presents this questioning of tradition as a good thing while also showing how Mr Birling is alarmed at being challenged by the younger generation.

Questions

QUICK TEST
1. What does Arthur show about the older generation at the start of the play?
2. What does Sheila show about the younger generation at the start of the play?
3. Why does Priestley make Sheila and Eric come into conflict with their parents?

EXAM PRACTICE
Using one or more of the 'Key Quotations to Learn', write a paragraph exploring the importance of generational conflict in the play.

Time

You must be able to: analyse how Priestley uses ideas about time in the play.

How is the play linked to its time?

By setting the play several decades before he was writing, Priestley can use time to explore key ideas about its characters and themes.

In particular, Arthur's confidence in the Titanic and the impossibility of war creates dramatic irony that signals to the audience he isn't as wise as he thinks.

The Inspector's final words about 'fire and blood and anguish' refer to the two world wars that took place between the play's setting and when it was written. This allows the audience to reflect on the past and how and why society has changed.

How does Priestley use time to structure the play?

The play takes place over one evening with each act leading directly into the next, intensifying the destruction of the Birlings' cosy, self-centred way of life.

The series of **flashbacks** over a two-year period, as told by the characters, present Eva's life as a continual struggle against inequality. This emphasises the idea of a chain of events, consequences and the fact they cannot change the past.

By the end, the play has almost come full circle. Arthur, Sybil and Gerald are feeling safe and secure when they receive news that a police inspector is on his way. Priestley does this to convey the idea that, unless people change, society is doomed to keep making the same mistakes. He creates an intriguing cliffhanger ending that explores the idea of second chances; the audience are left wondering how the characters will respond to the consequences of their actions a second time around.

How does time affect the mood on stage?

The Inspector talks about needing to hurry in Act 3 and the quickened pace raises the tension on stage. It also adds to the story's mystery as the audience later realise the Inspector needed to finish before the real police arrived.

The play shows the past returning to haunt the characters. This allows Priestley to create a range of atmospheres on stage, such as Sheila's distress at how her previous actions have affected a girl's future, Gerald's desperation to keep his past secret, Sybil's shock at her son's past and Arthur's fear of future scandal.

While Eric and Sheila regret the past, Arthur and Sybil want to deny it. The Inspector says the characters will never forget what they did.

Key Quotations to Learn

Inspector: 'A chain of events' (Act 1)

Inspector (to Sybil): 'you're going to spend the rest of your life regretting it' (Act 2)

Inspector: 'I haven't much time' (Act 3)

Summary

- The short time-scale intensifies the events on stage.
- The flashbacks create an idea of past events and their consequences.
- Different responses to the past allow Priestley to create different moods on stage.
- Eric and Sheila want to mend the past while Arthur and Sybil deny it.

Sample Analysis

Priestley explores time through the idea that the past affects the present. For example,

Sybil: Fine feelings and scruples that were simply absurd in a girl in her position.

Inspector: Her position now is that she lies with a burnt-out inside on a slab.

This dialogue expresses how Mrs Birling's past actions contributed to Eva Smith's suicide. Whereas Mrs Birling is dismissive of Eva, the Inspector's brutal description asserts that she doesn't give enough weight to the consequences of her actions. Priestley's message works on two levels: the consequences of individual actions and the need for society as a whole to build a better, more compassionate world.

Questions

QUICK TEST
1. How is the past used to show the audience something about Arthur?
2. What is the effect of setting the play over one evening?
3. Why does Priestley use flashbacks in the play?
4. How do Sheila and Eric respond to the past differently to Arthur and Sybil?

EXAM PRACTICE
Using one or more of the 'Key Quotations to Learn', write a paragraph exploring the importance of time in the play.

You must be able to: analyse how Priestley presents the theme of love.

How is love presented at the start of the play?

The play opens with the family celebrating Sheila and Gerald's engagement. The stage directions show that Sheila should talk '[*gaily*]' and in a '[*playful*]' manner and this presents love in a happy way.

They seem deeply in love when they look at each other during the toast and Gerald says, 'And I drink to you – and hope I can make you as happy as you deserve to be'.

However, the audience might notice possible uncertainty in the **verbs** 'hope' and 'deserve', while Sheila's reaction to the ring ('Now I feel really engaged') could imply that money plays a role in their love. This returns when we realise Arthur's own reasons for approving of their engagement.

How are men and love presented?

Love is presented as meaning different things to men and women.

For Sheila and Eva, it represents faithfulness. When describing Eva's feelings for him, Gerald says, 'I became at once the most important person in her life', and the superlative suggests constancy and attachment.

Love is also linked to romance for women, with Sheila using fairy tale **imagery** to describe how Eva must have felt towards Gerald, 'You were the wonderful Fairy Prince'.

However, the men see love differently with women being viewed as a commodity. Most obviously, Gerald has cheated on Sheila but expects her to resume their engagement at the end.

Gerald and Eric's relationships are both linked to sex more than love. Gerald admits about Eva, 'I didn't feel about her as she felt about me', and the relationship is ended within six months.

In particular, Eric says of Eva, 'she was pretty and a good sport'. The use of the word 'sport' suggests that Eric sees love as a game rather than a serious commitment.

How are marriage and love presented?

Linking to the gender inequality of the time, it is suggested that the values of the young men are passed down by their parents.

Arthur tries to defend Gerald's behaviour to Sheila and it is suggested that his married friends have affairs.

Sybil points out that men focus more on business than marriage but says that Sheila will 'have to get used to that, just as I had'.

Key Quotations to Learn

Gerald (about Eva): 'She told me she'd been happier than she'd ever been before – but that she knew it couldn't last' (Act 2)

Eric (about Eva): 'I wasn't in love with her or anything' (Act 3)

Gerald: 'Everything's alright now, Sheila. [*Holds up the ring.*] What about this ring?' (Act 3)

Summary

- Priestley presents Gerald and Sheila as being in love.
- However, Gerald has had an affair.
- Men and women are presented as having different views of love.
- The men are criticised for wanting sex more than love.

Sample Analysis

Priestley uses Gerald and Sheila to explore the idea of honesty in a relationship. In his reply to her question about Daisy Renton, 'All right. I knew her. Let's leave it at that', Gerald is hiding the truth from Sheila. Rather than any apology, he tries to close the discussion. This is also an assertion of male dominance, when he makes a decision for 'us', linking to attitudes of gender at the time. Gerald sees himself as beyond reproach; he thinks Sheila should not question his love but instead just accept whatever he says as the truth.

Questions

QUICK TEST
1. Where is marriage presented positively?
2. How does Sybil present a negative aspect of marriage?
3. What is different about men and women's attitudes to love in the play?
4. How is Eric's relationship with Eva presented as being about sex?

EXAM PRACTICE
Using one or more of the 'Key Quotations to Learn', write a paragraph exploring the importance of love in the play.

Tips and Assessment Objectives

You must be able to: understand how to approach the exam question and meet the requirements of the mark scheme.

Quick tips

- You will get a choice of two questions. Do the one that best matches your knowledge, the quotations you have learned and the things you have revised.

- Make sure you know what the question is asking you and underline key words to help keep you focused.

- You should spend about 50 minutes on your *An Inspector Calls* response. Allow yourself five minutes to plan your answer so there is a clear structure to your essay.

- All your paragraphs should contain a clearly explained idea about the play, a relevant reference to the play (ideally a quotation) and links to the play's context.

- It can sometimes help, after each paragraph, to quickly re-read the question to keep yourself focussed on the exam task.

- Keep your writing concise and aim for sophisticated expression.

- It is a good idea to remember what the mark scheme is asking of you...

AO1: Understand and respond to the play (16 marks)

This is all about coming up with a range of points that match the question, making clear interpretations of the play, supporting your ideas with references from the text and writing your essay in a mature, academic style.

Lower	Middle	Upper
The essay has some good ideas that are mostly relevant. Some quotations and references are used to support the ideas.	A clear essay that always focuses on the exam question. Quotations and references support ideas effectively. The response refers to different points in the play.	A convincing, well-structured essay that answers the question fully. Quotations and references are well-chosen and integrated into sentences. The response covers the whole play (not everything, but ideas from all three acts rather than just focussing on one or two sections).

AO3: Understand the relationship between the play and its contexts (16 marks)

For this part of the mark scheme, you need to show your understanding of how the characters or Priestley's ideas relate to when he was writing (1945) or when the play was set (1912).

Lower	Middle	Upper
Some awareness of how ideas in the play link to its context.	References to relevant aspects of context show a clear understanding.	Exploration is linked to specific aspects of the play's contexts to show a detailed understanding. Context is fully integrated.

AO4: Written accuracy (8 marks)

You need to use a range of accurate vocabulary, punctuation and spelling in order to convey your ideas clearly and effectively.

Lower	Middle	Upper
Reasonable level of accuracy. Errors do not get in the way of the essay making sense.	Good level of accuracy. Vocabulary and sentences help to keep ideas clear.	Consistent high level of accuracy. Vocabulary and sentences are used to make ideas clear and precise.

Practice Questions

1. **Gerald:** *We are respectful citizens and not criminals.*

    Inspector: *Sometimes there isn't as much difference as you think.*

    Explore the importance of morality in the play.

    You must refer to the context of the play in your answer.

2. **Sybil:** *That – I consider – is a trifle impertinent, Inspector.*

    Explore the significance of Sybil Birling in *An Inspector Calls.*

    You must refer to the context of the play in your answer.

3. **Sybil:** *As if a girl of that sort would ever refuse money.*

    Explore the importance of class differences in *An Inspector Calls.*

    You must refer to the context of the play in your answer.

4. **Arthur:** *There's a fair chance that I might find my way into the next Honours List. Just a knighthood, of course.*

    Explore the significance of Arthur Birling in the play.

    You must refer to the context of the play in your answer.

5. **Inspector:** *But each of you helped to kill her. Remember that. Never forget it.*

    Explore the importance of responsibility in *An Inspector Calls.*

    You must refer to the context of the play in your answer.

6. **Eric:** *You're beginning to pretend now that nothing's really happened.*

    Explore the significance of Eric in the play.

    You must refer to the context of the play in your answer.

7. **Eric:** *I don't give a damn now whether I stay here or not.*

    Explore the relationship between Eric and Arthur Birling in *An Inspector Calls.*

    You must refer to the context of the play in your answer.

8. **Sheila:** *I behaved badly too. I know I did. I'm ashamed of it.*

    In what ways is regret important in the play?

    You must refer to the context of the play in your answer.

9. **Inspector:** *We don't live alone. We are members of one body. We are responsible for each other.*

    Explore the significance of the Inspector in the play.

    You must refer to the context of the play in your answer.

10. **Sybil:** *I consider I did my duty.*

    In what ways are attitudes to duty important in *An Inspector Calls*?

    You must refer to the context of the play in your answer.

11. **Arthur:** *Why you hysterical young fool – get back – or I'll –*

    Explore how characters come into conflict in *An Inspector Calls.*

    You must refer to the context of the play in your answer.

12. **Inspector:** *It would do us all a bit of good if sometimes we tried to put ourselves in the place of these young women counting their pennies in their dingy little back bedrooms.*

    Explore the importance of inequality in the play.

    You must refer to the context of the play in your answer.

13. **Arthur:** *[heartily] Nonsense! You'll have a good laugh over it yet. Look, you'd better ask Gerald for that ring you gave back to him, hadn't you? Then you'll feel better.*

    Sheila: *[passionately] You're pretending everything's just as it was before.*

    In what ways are differences between children and parents important in *An Inspector Calls*?

    You must refer to the context of the play in your answer.

14. **Arthur:** *'a man has to mind his own business and look after himself'.*

    Explore the importance of self-interest in the play.

    You must refer to the context of the play in your answer.

15. **Sheila:** *You and I aren't the same people who sat down to dinner here.*

    Explore the relationship between Sheila and Gerald in *An Inspector Calls*.

    You must refer to the context of the play in your answer.

16. **Arthur:** *Haven't I already said there'll be a public scandal – unless we're lucky – and who here will suffer from that more than I will?*

    Explore the importance of respectability in *An Inspector Calls*.

    You must refer to the context of the play in your answer.

17. **Arthur:** *[angrily] And you'd better keep quiet anyhow. If that had been a police inspector and he'd heard you confess –*

    Sybil: *[warningly] Arthur – careful!*

    Arthur: *[hastily] Yes, yes.*

    Explore the relationship between Arthur and Sybil Birling in the play.

    You must refer to the context of the play in your answer.

18. **Sheila:** *You began to learn something. And now you've stopped.*

    Explore the significance of Sheila in *An Inspector Calls*.

    You must refer to the context of the play in your answer.

Planning a Character Question Response

You must be able to: understand what an exam question is asking you and prepare your response.

How might an exam question on character be phrased?

A typical character question will read like this:

Sheila: *You began to learn something. And now you've stopped.*

Explore the significance of Sheila in *An Inspector Calls*.

You must refer to the context of the play in your answer.

[40 marks, including 8 AO4 marks]

How do I work out what to do?

The focus of this question is clear: Sheila and her role in the play.

'Explore', 'significance' and 'context' are important elements of this question.

For AO1, these words show that you need to display a clear understanding of what Sheila is like and how this relates to the themes of the play and Priestley's intentions.

For AO3, you need to be linking your interpretations to the play's social, historical or literary context.

You also need to remember to write in an accurate and sophisticated way to achieve your 8 AO4 marks for spelling, punctuation, grammar and expression.

How can I plan my essay?

You have approximately 50 minutes to write your essay.

This isn't long but you should spend the first five minutes writing a quick plan. This will help you to focus your thoughts and produce a well-structured essay.

Try to come up with five or six ideas. Each of these ideas can then be written up as a paragraph.

You can plan in whatever way you find most useful. Some students like to just make a quick list of points and then re-number them into a logical order. Spider diagrams are particularly popular; look at the example on the opposite page.

In Act 1 seems self-satisfied, obedient. Follows traditional expectations of class and gender. Forms contrast with Eva to create a comment on the middle classes.
'[very pleased with life and rather excited]'

Significance of Sheila

Eventual guilt and understanding. Contrasts with parents to indicate that the younger generation can change. She understands the need for equality – link to world wars and possible revolution.
'began to learn something. And now you've stopped'
'Fire and blood and anguish'

Has Eva sacked out of jealousy and anger. Middle class lack understanding of working class. Theme of morality and literary tradition of morality play. Lack of Christian values.
'She was a very pretty girl too – and that didn't make it any better'

Growing guilt but resists personal responsibility, reflection on middle class and attitude to socialism.
'I know I'm to blame – and I'm desperately sorry – but I can't believe – I won't believe – it's simply my fault that in the end – she committed suicide'

Initial lack of guilt, based on selfishness and capitalist values. Link to Priestley's socialist values and looking back to a different time (1912).
'I feel I can never go there again'

Summary

- Make sure you know what the focus of the essay is.
- Remember to interpret the character: what does he/she represent and what ideas are being conveyed?
- Try to relate your ideas to the play's context and Priestley's intentions.

Questions

QUICK TEST

1. What key skills do you need to show in your answer?
2. What are the benefits of quickly planning your essay?
3. Why do you need to take care with your writing?

EXAM PRACTICE

Plan a response to the following exam question:

Eric: *You're beginning to pretend now that nothing's really happened.*

Explore the significance of Eric in the play.

You must refer to the context of the play in your answer. [40 marks, including 8 AO4 marks]

Grade 5 Annotated Response

Sheila: *You began to learn something. And now you've stopped.*

Explore the significance of Sheila in *An Inspector Calls*.

You must refer to the context of the play in your answer. [40 marks, including 8 AO4 marks]

Sheila is a significant character in An Inspector Calls as Priestley uses her to explore different themes and ideas about society [1].

The stage directions at the start of the play tell us that Sheila is self-satisfied. 'very pleased'. This is because she has just got engaged to Gerald. She does not work and she is obedient to her parents [2]. Priestley establishes Sheila as a typical daughter of a wealthy middle class family, following the social expectations at the time [3]. Sheila is like the opposite of Eva Smith who is poor and lonely and represents the working class at the time [4].

Sheila is important in the fate of Eva Smith because it is her fault that she is sacked from Milwards. Sheila has Eva sacked because she is in a bad mood and is jealous of her prettiness. This links to the play's theme of morality because Sheila's behaviour is cruel and unfair [5]. This shows how powerful the middle class were because shops needed their money so if they weren't happy the shop would do what they wanted, like sacking someone. It shows that some people really didn't care about what happened to the poor as long as they were happy themselves. The play is set in 1912 which was before the growth of socialism so Priestley is showing how different and bad things were in the past [6].

Sheila's guilt is an important part of the play. In comparison, her parents don't feel guilty. At first, she is selfish. This is because of the way she has been brought up and she moans that she can't go to Milwards anymore. 'I feel I can never go there again'. This shows she doesn't really feel guilty because she is thinking about herself and her life being worse rather than thinking about Eva Smith and how her life is over because she committed suicide. This is all about the values of the middle class being bad and how they just wanted more and more money [7].

Sheila is different by the end of the play because she has accepted full responsibility so Priestley is suggesting that people can change. Sheila is a contrast to Mr and Mrs Birling who still have the same attitudes so Priestley is saying that it is the younger generation who can change. 'You began to learn something. And now you've stopped'. She actually challenges her parents unlike at the start of the play. She has changed her values and wants her parents to do the same. She understands that it is important to care about the working class which shows that she has listened to what the Inspector has been saying and has learnt from him. She even repeats his words at the end as if she is becoming a bit socialist and will grow up better than her parents [8].

Sheila is a significant character. She shows what middle class people were like and how they could change [9].

1. A basic introduction that would benefit from more specific details about theme and intention. AO1

2. Clear ideas about Sheila's character that would benefit from stronger textual evidence. The quotation should be embedded. AO1

3. Relevant links to social context, although the actual time could be specified more clearly. AO3

4. Some interpretation of Sheila's character; Priestley's intentions could be explored more clearly. AO1/AO3

5. Some interpretation of Sheila's character with a fairly clear textual reference, although a fully embedded quotation would be better. AO1

6. Some good social context and acknowledgement of Priestley's intentions. It could be written in a more concise way with stronger links to the interpretation of Sheila's character. AO1/AO3/AO4

7. There is some interpretation of Sheila's character. This is supported by a clear, but not embedded, quotation. Context is used to develop the point. Writing is fairly accurate but sentences could be constructed more carefully and vocabulary could be more precise and sophisticated. AO1/AO3/AO4

8. Although it could be expressed in a more sophisticated way, there is clear interpretation of Sheila's character. It is supported by textual evidence, making good use of the exam question, and there is an attempt to integrate context. AO1/AO3/AO4

9. A basic conclusion that could be developed further. AO1/AO3

Questions

EXAM PRACTICE

Choose a paragraph from this essay. Read it through a few times then try to rewrite and improve it. You might:

- Improve the sophistication of the language or the clarity of expression.
- Replace a reference with a quotation.
- Ensure quotations are embedded in the sentence.
- Provide a clearer interpretation of Sheila's character.
- Link context to the interpretation more effectively.

Grade 7+ Annotated Response

A proportion of the best top-band answers will be awarded Grade 8 or Grade 9. To achieve this, you should aim for a sophisticated, fluent and nuanced response that displays flair and originality.

Sheila: *You began to learn something. And now you've stopped.*

Explore the significance of Sheila in *An Inspector Calls*.

You must refer to the context of the play in your answer. [40 marks, including 8 AO4 marks]

Sheila's significance in the play comes from the way Priestley uses the character to expose what he saw as the social irresponsibility of the middle classes as well as his hope that the younger generation can bring about change [1].

Sheila is initially presented as self-satisfied. Stage directions suggest she should be performed as '[very pleased with life and rather excited]', she does not work, is obedient to her parents, and her reference to them as 'Mummy and Daddy' indicates some childishness [2]. Priestley establishes Sheila as a typical daughter of a wealthy middle class family, following the social expectations of class and gender in the early twentieth century [3]. He does this to create a contrast with the life of working class girls like Eva Smith, later described as 'counting their pennies in their dingy little back bedrooms', to highlight the theme of inequality [4].

In terms of narrative, Sheila is important in the fate of Eva Smith as she has her sacked from Milwards. Drawing on the literary genre of the morality play, Sheila represents envy and wrath, 'She was a very pretty girl too – and that didn't make it any better', angrily complaining about Eva because she is jealous of her prettiness [5]. Priestley is pointing out the hypocrisy of a Christian society that does not follow Christian values. He is also showing the power of the middle classes and their lack of awareness of the precarious nature of working class lives. Writing in 1945, Priestley is looking back to a time before class structures began to erode, before the rise of socialism, and before the suffragette movement started to achieve female equality and sisterhood, allowing him to indirectly celebrate modern social changes [6].

Sheila's guilt, in comparison with her parents, is a key feature of the play. At first, she displays the selfishness that she has been brought up with, commenting that she cannot now return to Milwards. Her line, 'I feel I can never go there again', could also link to how her family values have been established through the capitalist ideals which were dominant at the start of the twentieth century: she is more concerned about material goods than the life of a young woman [7].

Although her guilt increases, her feelings are still mixed. When she says, 'I know I'm to blame – and I'm desperately sorry – but I can't believe – I won't believe – it's simply my fault', Priestley shows someone who is unwilling to take ultimate personal responsibility. She rejects the socialist values that the Inspector later summarises as 'We are members of one body. We are responsible for each other', but it is also clear that she is struggling with her conscience in a way that her parents do not, introducing Priestley's assertion that the young can change [8].

This change comes towards the end of the play where Sheila accepts full responsibility, in contrast to her parents. She points out that they, 'began to learn something. And now you've stopped', showing that she has changed her values and wants them to do the same. She will not return to her traditional and materialistic way of life, symbolised by the way she doesn't take back Gerald's ring. When she repeats the Inspector's words, 'Fire and blood and anguish', it underlines the idea that she has understood his warning about the need for social change. Priestley is making a reference to the two world wars, to highlight some of the reasons why class and inequality had begun to change, but it can also be an image of revolution with Sheila understanding the possible consequences of the wealthy not caring about the working classes [9].

Sheila is a significant character as Priestley uses her to illustrate middle class selfishness and prejudice, while also celebrating how people can change. Placed in 1912, Sheila can be seen as the start of a new generation, breaking away from traditional beliefs and ways of life in order to pave the way for the socialist politics that Priestley believed could improve Britain [10].

1. Clear overview of Sheila's character. AO1
2. Clear ideas about Sheila's character, supported by embedded textual evidence. AO1
3. Relevant links to social context. AO3
4. Interpretation of Sheila's character and what Priestley is trying to achieve. AO1/AO3
5. Interpretation of character integrated evidence and literary context. AO1/AO3
6. Interpretation of Sheila's importance integrated with social context and Priestley's intentions. AO1/AO3
7. This paragraph is a good example of accurate and varied writing to make points effectively. This includes fully punctuated sentence structures, integrated quotations, discourse markers, and precise complex vocabulary. AO4
8. The essay explores the importance of more complex aspects of Sheila's character. AO1
9. Clear interpretation of Sheila's character, supported by integrated textual evidence and historical context. Good use of quotation from the exam question. AO1/AO3
10. Clear conclusion linked to historical context and Priestley's intentions. AO1/AO3

Questions

EXAM PRACTICE
Spend 50 minutes writing an answer to the following question:
Eric: *You're beginning to pretend now that nothing's really happened.*
Explore the significance of Eric in the play.
You must refer to the context of the play in your answer.
[40 marks, including 8 AO4 marks]
Remember to use the plan you have already prepared.

Planning a Theme Question Response

You must be able to: understand what an exam question is asking you and prepare your response.

How might an exam question on a theme be phrased?

A typical theme question will read like this:

Sybil: *As if a girl of that sort would ever refuse money.*

Explore the importance of attitudes towards the working class in *An Inspector Calls*.

You must refer to the context of the play in your answer.

How do I work out what to do?

The focus of this question is clear: different attitudes towards the working class in the play.

'Explore', 'importance' and 'context' are important elements of this question.

For AO1, these words show that you need to display a clear understanding of what attitudes are displayed towards the working class and how these relate to the themes of the play and Priestley's intentions.

For AO3, you need to be linking your interpretations to the play's social, historical or literary context.

You also need to remember to write in an accurate and sophisticated way to achieve your eight AO4 marks for spelling, punctuation, grammar and expression.

How can I plan my essay?

You have approximately 50 minutes to write your essay.

This isn't long but you should spend the first five minutes writing a quick plan. This will help you to focus your thoughts and produce a well-structured essay.

Try to come up with five or six ideas. Each of these ideas can then be written up as a paragraph.

You can plan in whatever way you find most useful. Some students like to just make a quick list of points and then re-number them in a logical order. Spider diagrams are particularly popular; look at the example on the opposite page.

Arthur and Gerald see working class as less important. They are just a resource for making money. Link to Priestley's beliefs in socialism and equality.
'it's my duty to keep labour costs down'

Arthur's distrust of the working class. Believes that equality will reduce the quality of life of the middle classes. 1912 labour strikes.
'If you don't come down sharply on these people, they'd soon be asking for the earth'

Inspector's view to contrast with Mr and Mrs Birling. Link to socialism and the creation of the welfare state. Sheila and Eric changing to agree with the Inspector shows hope for the younger generation. Reference to war shows working class have earned the right to equality.
'We don't live alone. We are members of one body. We are responsible for each other'
'fire and blood and anguish'

Importance of attitude towards the working class

Sybil's snobbery and prejudice. Belief that the working class are less important and lack morality. Irony of Christian charities without Christian values.
'As if a girl of that sort would ever refuse money'

Summary

- Make sure you know what the focus of the essay is.
- Remember to interpret the theme: how is it shown and what ideas are being conveyed?
- Try to relate your ideas to the play's context and Priestley's intentions.

Questions

QUICK TEST
1. What key skills do you need to show in your answer?
2. What are the benefits of quickly planning your essay?
3. Why do you need to take care with your writing?

EXAM PRACTICE
Plan a response to the following exam question:
Eric: *It's what happened to the girl and what we all did to her that matters.*
Explore the importance of guilt in *An Inspector Calls*.
You must refer to the context of the play in your answer.
[40 marks, including 8 AO4 marks]

Sybil: *As if a girl of that sort would ever refuse money.*

Explore the importance of attitudes towards the working class in *An Inspector Calls.*

You must refer to the context of the play in your answer.

[40 marks, including 8 AO4 marks]

Priestley shows different attitudes towards the working class through the characters in the play. Because he is writing about the past, Priestley is showing that things have changed [1].

In Act 1, Priestley uses Arthur and Gerald to represent traditional middle class attitudes towards the working class. Arthur believes that working class people are just there to work in factories. He thinks they shouldn't be paid much and that they need to be kept in their place [2]. He doesn't see them as the same as him. They are different to middle class businessmen who he thinks are better. This shows the need for equality which was starting when Priestley wrote the play [3].

Arthur also distrusts the working class. 'If you don't come down sharply on these people, they'd soon be asking for the earth'. He thinks they must be treated harshly or they will get above themselves and this would take money away from the middle class and cause their lives to be less luxurious. This links to the fact there were lots of labour strikes in 1912. Priestley was all for this because it could bring about equality. However, Birling is worried that the working class will start to be expensive and so his factory won't make as much profit. Gerald agrees with him which shows that this view was widespread among the middle class, it's not just Arthur thinking these things [4].

Priestley also uses Sybil to show that the middle class were really snobby about the working class and looked down on them like they were dirt and when she talks about Eva Smith she shows no sympathy or respect. It's like she thinks they are less important, almost like animals rather than people [5]. Sybil's view is wrong because the working class are good people and Eva Smith seemed really nice. Priestley shows Sybil up because she runs a charity that is linked to the church but she doesn't actually show any values of a religious person, she just judges people even though it's her who needs to be judged for looking down on innocent people like Eva Smith [6].

Priestley also includes the viewpoint of the Inspector as it's different to the viewpoint of the Birlings and suggests that the working class need to be treated better. This is the same as Priestley's socialist values which were around when the play was written. 'We don't live alone. We are members of one body. We are responsible for each other'. This is the attitude that society needs to unite and look after its less fortunate groups. In 1945 they set up the welfare state [7].

Overall, the play starts by showing traditional attitudes towards the working classes. Then it shows the Inspector's view which is better. Instead of being selfish and seeing the working class as slaves, we should be compassionate and try to make everyone equal [8].

1. Basic introduction. Ideas about attitudes could be more specific. There is a useful but vague link to historical context. AO1/AO3

2. A fairly clear interpretation of attitudes towards the working class. It would benefit from stronger textual evidence. AO1

3. Relevant but rather vague links to social context. AO3

4. Some interpretation of attitudes but ideas could be more clearly expressed. Strong evidence is included but could be integrated into the sentence. There is a generally successful attempt to link interpretation to historical context and consideration of what Priestley is trying to achieve. AO1/AO3

5. Some development of exploration through a new viewpoint, although the quotation from the exam question could be used to provide evidence. AO1

6. Writing is fairly accurate but sentences could be constructed more carefully. Vocabulary could be more precise and sophisticated, and there is too much repetition. AO4

7. Interpretation of a different viewpoint to add depth to the essay. Evidence is included but could be integrated more effectively. There are links to Priestley's aims and social/historical context but some of this is tagged on rather than being linked to the interpretation. AO1/AO3

8. Clear but basic conclusion that identifies the message of the play. AO1

 Questions

EXAM PRACTICE
Choose a paragraph from this essay. Read it through a few times then try to rewrite and improve it. You might:
- Improve the sophistication of the language or the clarity of expression.
- Replace a reference with a quotation.
- Ensure quotations are embedded in the sentence.
- Provide a clearer interpretation of attitudes towards the working class.
- Link context to the interpretation more effectively.

Grade 7+ Annotated Response

A proportion of the best top-band answers will be awarded Grade 8 or Grade 9. To achieve this, you should aim for a sophisticated, fluent and nuanced response that displays flair and originality.

Sybil: *As if a girl of that sort would ever refuse money.*

Explore the importance of attitudes towards the working class in *An Inspector Calls*.

You must refer to the context of the play in your answer.

[40 marks, including 8 AO4 marks]

Priestley criticises a lack of empathy for the working class through the attitudes of the Birlings, contrasting their viewpoint with those of the Inspector. Writing in 1945, at the time of a new socialist government, Priestley looks back to 1912 to show the importance of social change.

In Act 1, Priestley uses Arthur and Gerald to represent traditional middle class attitudes towards the working class. When Arthur says, 'it's my duty to keep labour costs down', he represents the viewpoint that the working class are there to be exploited and need to be kept in their place [2]. He sees them as a different group of people, in comparison to middle class businessmen, and Priestley uses this to assert the importance of new socialist ideas about equality [3].

Arthur is also used to show the idea that the working class are distrusted. He argues that, 'If you don't come down sharply on these people, they'd soon be asking for the earth', implying that they should be treated harshly in order to safeguard the privileges of the middle class. Priestley is drawing on the labour strikes of 1912 and using the audience's dislike of Birling to suggest the value of industrial action in order to achieve greater rights and fair pay. During Birling's speeches, Gerald's agreement is used to make it clear that the audience are listening to a majority view rather than an isolated opinion [4].

As well as showing how the working class were viewed as an exploitable resource, Priestley uses Sybil to convey the prejudice and snobbery that many of the middle class displayed towards the working class. In Act 2, she says of Eva Smith, 'as if a girl of that sort would ever refuse money!', suggesting she has no sympathy or respect for the working class because they are of a different breed [5]. This implies the working class were seen as lacking proper morals and Priestley uses the irony of Sybil's lack of Christian values to point out the hypocrisy of church-based charities (like the one Sybil chairs) that claimed to help the poor but actually sat in judgement on them [6].

Through the Inspector, Priestley challenges these attitudes and offers an alternative view that the working class need to be treated better. Reflecting the socialist views that were gathering popularity in the early 20th century, the Inspector says, 'We don't live alone. We are members of one body. We are responsible for each other', emphasising the need for society to unite and look after its less fortunate groups. This notion could be particularly seen, at the time the play was written, in the establishing of the welfare state [7]. The way in which Sheila and Eric change their attitudes towards the working class to show compassion is used by Priestley to represent hope for the future and the importance of educating and mobilising the younger generation [8].

Overall, the play establishes traditional attitudes towards the working classes, uses the story of Eva Smith to show their damaging consequences, and then offers a better alternative. First performed after World War Two, the Inspector's emotive reference to 'fire and blood and anguish' reminds the audience of the role the working classes played in maintaining the wealth and freedom of the rest of society, thereby highlighting the rightfulness of social equality to the audience, not just to the characters on stage [9].

1. Clear overview of attitudes towards the working class, incorporating historical context. AO1/AO3

2. Clear interpretation of attitudes towards the working class, supported by embedded textual evidence. AO1

3. Relevant links to social context. AO3

4. Interpretation of attitudes, supported by an embedded quotation, integrated with historical context and consideration of what Priestley is trying to achieve. AO1/AO3

5. Good development of exploration through a new viewpoint, making effective use of the quotation from the exam question. AO1

6. This paragraph is a good example of accurate and varied writing to make points effectively. This includes fully punctuated sentence structures, integrated quotations, discourse markers, and precise complex vocabulary. AO4

7. Interpretation of a different viewpoint to add depth to the essay. Textual evidence, Priestley's aims and social/historical context are well integrated. AO1/AO3

8. Reference to other characters is used to develop ideas further. AO1

9. Clear conclusion, supported by another embedded quotation, is linked to historical context and Priestley's intentions. AO1/AO3

> ## Questions
>
> EXAM PRACTICE
> Spend 50 minutes writing an answer to the following question:
> Eric: *It's what happened to the girl and what we all did to her that matters.*
> Explore the importance of guilt in *An Inspector Calls*.
> You must refer to the context of the play in your answer.
> [40 marks, including 8 AO4 marks]
> Remember to use the plan you have already prepared.

Glossary

Atmosphere – the mood or emotion in a play.

Capitalist – a right-wing political belief in individual gain, through hard work and a focus on profit.

Cliffhanger – ending an act with a shock or problem.

Climax – the most intense part of an act or the whole play.

Compassion – sympathetic concern.

Confession – a statement admitting guilt; (in religion) acknowledging sin.

Conflict – a disagreement or argument.

Conscience – a person's sense of right and wrong.

Convention – an expected way in which something is usually done.

Depression (economic) – when less spending causes businesses to close and unemployment to rise, leading to even less spending.

Dominance – having power and influence over others.

Dramatic irony – when the audience of a play is aware of something that a character on stage isn't.

Emotive – creating or describing strong emotions.

Etiquette – a code of polite behaviour in society.

Exploited – used in an unfair way (for the user's benefit).

Flashback – a dramatic device taking a play back in time.

Foreshadow – hint at future events in the play.

Hierarchy – a ranking according to status and power.

Hoax – a humorous or nasty trick.

Hypocrisy – claiming to have better standards or behaviour than is true.

Illegitimate – a person whose parents aren't married.

Imagery – words used to create a picture in the imagination.

Industrial Revolution – a period when machinery started to be used much more in production, leading to big factories rather than small businesses.

Inferior – being less important than others.

Irony – something that seems the opposite of what was expected; deliberately using words that mean the opposite of what is intended.

Justified – something done for a good, fair reason.

Juxtapose – place two contrasting things side by side.

Noun – an object or thing.

Objective – not influenced by personal feelings or opinions.

Omniscient – all-knowing.

Parallelism – repeating similar word orders or sentence constructions to emphasise an idea.

Passive voice – where the subject of a sentence has something done to it (in contrast to active voice, where the subject of the sentence does something).

Patriarch – the male head of a family.

Prejudiced – being against someone because of an already-formed idea, rather than fact or experience.

Provincial – living beyond a major city, suggesting a lack of sophistication.

Respectable – seen as good and proper by society.

Sin – an immoral act.

Strike – when workers refuse to work as a form of protest.

Suburb – a (usually quite well-off) residential area on the outskirts of a town or city.

Superior – being better or more important than others.

Symbolise – when an object or colour represents a specific idea or meaning.

Tension – a feeling of anticipation, discomfort, or excitement in a play.

Traditional – long-established or old-fashioned.

Verb – a doing or action word.

Welfare state – a system in which the government looks after the poor and vulnerable in society.

Womanising – having various casual affairs with women.

Answers

Pages 4–5
Quick Test
1. Arthur and Sybil, and their children, Eric and Sheila.
2. Sheila's engagement to Gerald Croft.
3. To investigate the suicide of a young girl, Eva Smith.
4. Eva worked at Arthur's factory and was sacked after helping to organise a strike in demand of higher wages.
5. Arthur thinks the sacking was justified and Gerald agrees. Eric and the Inspector show sympathy for Eva's situation.

Exam Practice
Answers might explore how the Birlings' happiness contrasts with Eva's death, suggesting the differences between middle class and working class life; the Inspector's interruption could represent the need for the middle classes to be more aware of the people around them.

Pages 6–7
Quick Test
1. Sheila feels sorry for Eva.
2. She thought Eva was laughing at her. She was in a bad mood and jealous of her looks.
3. She's upset about Eva, which shows some guilt, but she's also upset for herself and how her evening has been spoiled, which highlights the selfish side of her character.
4. Gerald.
5. She was having an affair with Gerald.

Exam Practice
Answers might explore Sheila's unwillingness to accept responsibility and Gerald's attempt to avoid responsibility, linking to selfish attitudes of the middle class and the lack of interest in equality.

Pages 8–9
Quick Test
1. To hide his involvement from the Inspector and possibly hide further details from Sheila.
2. She refers to her lower-class status.
3. She acts in a grand and superior manner.
4. Sybil is behaving how the others behaved before the Inspector exposed them.
5. It started as him innocently helping her but then they became lovers.

Exam Practice
Answers might explore Sybil's prejudice against Eva, representing traditional attitudes held by the middle classes; Gerald and the Inspector convey the inequality that the working class suffered, linking to the need for sympathy and welfare.

Pages 10–11
Quick Test
1. She was using the false name Mrs Birling.
2. No, she thinks it was justified.
3. Sheila thinks it was horrible; Arthur worries it might make them look bad.
4. She thought Eva was lying about the lover offering money but her refusing because she thought it was stolen.
5. Sheila works out that Eric is the father of Eva's child before her parents do.

Exam Practice
Answers might explore Sybil's prejudice against the working class and the irony of her lack of Christian values despite running a Christian charity; Sheila could represent the need to change.

Pages 12–13
Quick Test
1. He gets drunk and aggressive.
2. She knew he didn't love her.
3. Murdering Eva along with her own grandchild.
4. He wants to cover up the evening's revelations.
5. That we are all responsible for each other in society and change must come.

Exam Practice
Answers might explore the traditional patriarchal power shown by Arthur, as well as his abuse of economic power; the Inspector presents the idea of using such economic power to solve inequality.

Pages 14–15
Quick Test
1. They want to avoid any scandal.
2. Their sense of responsibility for Eva's death.
3. Relieved with a sense that things can go back to normal. They make a joke of it all.
4. They still know that, individually, they ruined a girl's life.
5. A phone call reveals that a girl has been found dead and an inspector is coming to interview them.

Exam Practice
Answers might explore how Sheila's viewpoint contrasts with her father's, suggesting that change will come through the younger generations.

Pages 16–17
Quick Test
1. There's only one set, the play takes place (without changes in time between the Acts) over one evening and characters are generally focussed on one at a time.
2. Use of cliffhangers to raise tension.
3. Character confessions lower the tension whilst family conflict raises it.
4. His social message about having personal and social responsibility.

Exam Practice
Answers might explore how mystery is used to gradually deconstruct and criticise the values of this middle class family.

Pages 18–19

Quick Test

1. Gerald Croft.
2. The Birlings.
3. Working class.
4. Capitalist. He is a businessman and focuses on making money.

Exam Practice

Answers might explore how the pause before Lady Croft's name, the use of her title and the defence of her snobbery shows Arthur's respect for the upper classes and his wish to be like them. As a capitalist, he believes in the importance of money and status. We also know, from Act 1, that he hopes a marriage between the Crofts and the Birlings will help to improve his business and his social position. He points out that the Crofts are from an old, land-owning family, reminding us that Birling represents the new wealth of the middle classes benefitting from the Industrial Revolution. He boasts about the possibility of the Honours List and a knighthood, showing that he sees a title as a way to become equal in status if not breeding.

Pages 20–21

Quick Test

1. The Inspector represents Priestley's socialist views about looking after everyone in society.
2. Fighting alongside men of all different classes may have influenced Priestley's belief in equality.
3. They established the welfare state, the National Health Service and new housing plans where people of different classes would live side by side.

Exam Practice

Arthur's noun phrase 'steadily increasing prosperity' would seem ironic given the economic depression that followed the First World War. The capitalist comments would also have conflicted with the growth of trade unions and the popularity of socialism after the Second World War, signalled by the Labour Party's landslide election win in 1945.

Pages 22–23

Quick Test

1. There was no social security or free health care.
2. Home, workplace, church and government.
3. Women were seen as unequal to men and were expected to stay at home and bring up a family, they had less access to jobs and promotion and had fewer legal rights.

Exam Practice

Answers might explore how Arthur is critical of sex outside of marriage, which links to Christian values; Eric's ironic adjective 'respectable' when discussing Arthur's friends who have affairs suggest that the double standards of the middle classes, often ignoring their own immoral behaviour to focus on criticising others; how this is emphasised when Arthur interrupts Eric to keep him quiet; the implication that women are less moral (and less important) than men.

Pages 24–25

Quick Test

1. The furniture, the glasses, the cigar box.
2. It isn't very cosy or homely.
3. The lighting is warm, the props suggest quality or luxury and the characters are sitting down.
4. The lighting becomes brighter and harder, to emphasise that they are being interrogated and exposed by the Inspector.

Exam Practice

Answers might focus on the look of the furniture and how it suggests both wealth and self-confidence, the size of the room and the expensive props such as champagne glasses or how the wealthy characters are seated whilst the maid clears up after them.

Pages 26–27

Quick Test

1. People in society should care for each other.
2. He doesn't show respect for the Birlings' higher status.
3. Goole/ghoul suggests mystery and perhaps the idea that the Inspector isn't 'real'.
4. He reveals their secrets and their bad behaviour, challenging their view of themselves.

Exam Practice

Answers might explore how the Inspector represents Priestley's belief in socialism, standing up to the traditional power of the middle classes and encouraging equality.

Pages 28–29

Quick Test

1. To establish his dominant character and his status as the head of the family.
2. 'hard-headed business man'.
3. He hopes it will link his factory with Croft's factory and improve his social status.
4. Because we know there was a war two years later, it shows he isn't as clever as he thinks and doesn't really understand society/the world.

Exam Practice

Answers might explore how Arthur represents capitalism and the traditional views of the middle classes, seeing the working class as a resource to be exploited; Priestley suggests that his wish to pass on these views to the younger generation should be resisted.

Pages 30–31

Quick Test

1. She usually takes Arthur's lead & follows his instructions.
2. Because she believes she lives a moral life and she thinks her wealth and social status make her more important. She draws on Arthur's status to support this.
3. She's a hypocrite. She pretends to care but just likes to judge.
4. She treats him like a child, doesn't understand his feelings and is unaware of his problems.

Exam Practice

Answers might explore how Sybil represents prejudice and snobbery against the working classes; she feels that their problems are their own and sees no social responsibility to help; she sees herself as better and believes, despite the evidence, that her children are better simply because they are middle class.

Pages 32–33

Quick Test

1. She is the daughter of a wealthy businessman and is dating a man from an upper-class family.
2. She thinks she is being laughed at, is in a bad mood and is jealous of Eva's prettiness.
3. She begins to accept her responsibility and sympathise with Eva's life.
4. Sheila realises that Eric was the father of Eva's child.

Answers

Pages 32–33 continued

Exam Practice

Answers might explore how Sheila represents a change of values; despite an initial unwillingness to accept responsibility, she recognises her guilt and encourages the older generation to change.

Pages 34–35

Quick Test

1. He isn't paired with another character (like Arthur/ Sybil and Sheila/Gerald) so seems isolated, he is the last to speak and he behaves strangely.
2. He thinks they had every right to go on strike and his father treated them badly.
3. He is ashamed.
4. He dislikes them and feels they've never tried to understand him.

Exam Practice

Answers might explore how Eric represents a change in values, turning against the traditions and hypocrisy of middle class society to see the need for equality and welfare.

Pages 36–37

Quick Test

1. He refers to himself as 'respectable' and has hidden his affair from his fiancée.
2. Arthur appreciates Gerald as a businessman but is more interested in his social status as a member of the upper classes.
3. He gave her food and found her somewhere to live.
4. He started an affair with her and then broke her heart.

Exam Practice

Answers might explore how Gerald represents middle class arrogance and the wish to avoid social and personal responsibility; his change of values is only temporary.

Pages 38–39

Quick Test

1. The working class and women.
2. Arthur sacks her for wanting more money, Sheila has her sacked unfairly, Gerald helps her but then makes her his lover and breaks her heart, Eric gets her pregnant and Sybil refuses to help her.
3. She is hardworking (as opposed to Sheila and Eric) and she refuses to take Eric's money once she thinks it is stolen.
4. Edna's role as a servant shows that the Birlings are happy to employ people to fulfil their needs; the idea of having some below them, in a position of inequality, does not trouble them.

Exam Practice

Answers might explore how the life of working class people is presented by the Inspector in order to emphasise the need for equality and the importance of socialist values.

Pages 40–41

Quick Test

1. Public scandal.
2. Eric and Sheila accept their guilt and know they need to change; their parents refuse to accept any responsibility.
3. He asks her to take the engagement ring again.
4. Their lack of closeness and understanding has now been exposed and their relationship has deteriorated.

Exam Practice

Answers might explore how the older generation are unwilling to change, wanting to cling on to tradition and power; their selfishness is contrasted with the willingness of the young to see the importance of different, more compassionate values.

Page 42–43

Quick Test

1. His wish for more money and status.
2. He used Eva for sexual gratification and he drinks too much.
3. Eva's prettiness.
4. When she refers to her status or her belief that she has the right to judge others.

Exam Practice

Answers might explore how Priestley exposes the hypocrisy and immorality of the middle class; despite seeing themselves as better, they display jealousy, pride, and desire; they don't care for the life of an individual, they care for themselves.

Pages 44–45

Quick Test

1. Eric and Gerald.
2. It interrupts Arthur's promotion of self-interest.
3. Her life is ruined because people followed their own interests not hers.
4. He points out the irony of them, given what the Inspector exposed.

Exam Practice

Answers might explore how Arthur's traditional capitalist values lack compassion, whereas the Inspector's socialist values suggest a responsibility for society and the importance of equality.

Pages 46–47

Quick Test

1. Offer financial, emotional and educational support.
2. It's nonsense.
3. She does charitable work but it is to make her look good; she looks down on the girls who ask for help.

Exam Practice

Answers might explore how the Inspector represents ideas of empathy and helping others; he embodies ideas of the new welfare state at the time Priestley was writing; in contrast, Arthur thinks such views are ridiculous and self-interest is more important.

Pages 48–49

Quick Test

1. Sheila, Eric and – to some extent – Gerald.
2. 'Confess'.
3. Deny involvement and blame others.

Exam Practice

Answers might explore how the Inspector encourages the characters to take personal responsibility; the younger generation accept this while the older generation avoid it, considering themselves beyond judgement.

Pages 50–51

Quick Test

1. Because she is working class and a woman.
2. Their home, their money, Eric's education and Arthur's status.
3. Being able to keep labour costs down means that the family business makes more money.

Exam Practice

Answers might explore how the characters display contrasting views of inequality; Arthur sees it as a good thing, believing in capitalist values of profit and self-interest, whereas Sheila recognises that the working class are more than just a resource - they are individuals; it can be argued that Gerald takes advantage of his economic superiority to fulfill his sexual desires.

Pages 52–53

Quick Test

1. They expect to be in charge.
2. They follow social expectations of respect for their elders.
3. To show that the older generation have old-fashioned views that are harmful to society as a whole, whereas the young people can change and contribute to a better future.

Exam Practice

Answers might explore how the play begins with the younger generation showing traditional obedience to the older generation, but later shows the values of the older generation being challenged.

Pages 54–55

Quick Test

1. By setting the play in the past, we can see that Arthur isn't as wise as he thinks.
2. It intensifies the situation and the emotions or tension being created.
3. To emphasise particular events and their consequences.
4. Sheila and Eric admit and want to remedy the past, whereas Arthur and Sybil want to deny and conceal the past.

Exam Practice

Answers might explore how the play focuses on the consequences of actions and the urgent need for social change; written in 1945 and looking back to 1912, there is the constant sense of changes to come and the effects of the two world wars.

Pages 56–57

Quick Test

1. At the start of the play with the happy engagement party.
2. Telling Sheila she'll have to get used to her husband putting work before his marriage.
3. Women appear to value faithfulness and romance more than men. Gerald has an affair and then dumps Eva, Arthur appears to think unfaithfulness is easy to forgive and Eric uses Eva for his sexual pleasure.
4. Eric says he didn't love her, she was just good fun.

Exam Practice

Answers might explore how men are shown to exploit women in the name of love, seeing them as trophies or sexual objects; there is a lack of actual love in the play, with the men often presenting economic power as a substitute for love.

Pages 60–61

Practice Questions

Use the mark scheme on page 80 to self-assess your strengths and weaknesses. The estimated grade boundaries are included so you can assess your progress towards your target grade.

Pages 62–63

Quick Test

1. Understanding of the whole text, use of textual evidence, awareness of the relevance of context, a well-structured essay and accurate writing.
2. Planning focuses your thoughts and allows you to produce a well-structured essay.
3. There are 8 marks available for using a range of accurate vocabulary, punctuation, and spelling in order to convey your ideas clearly and effectively.

Exam Practice

Answers might explore Eric's initial portrayal as a lazy and spoiled member of the middle class; his lack of morality undermines the family's idea that they are better than the working class; he is used to expose the hypocrisy of the middle class through the abuses of power and money that he reveals; Eric is also a symbol of hope that the younger generation can change; he begins to display socialist values, caring about the lives of others and wanting to stop inequality.

Pages 66–67 and pages 72–73

Exam Practice

Use the mark scheme on page 80 to self-assess your strengths and weaknesses. Work up from the bottom, putting a tick by things you have fully accomplished, a ½ by skills that are in place but need securing, and underlining areas that need particular development. The estimated grade boundaries are included so you can assess your progress towards your target grade.

Pages 68–69

Quick Test

1. Understanding of the whole text, use of textual evidence, awareness of the relevance of context, a well-structured essay and accurate writing.
2. Planning focuses your thoughts and allows you to produce a well-structured essay.
3. There are 8 marks available for using a range of accurate vocabulary, punctuation, and spelling in order to convey your ideas clearly and effectively.

Exam Practice

Answers might explore the Inspector's attempt to get the Birlings to acknowledge their guilt, linking to socialist ideas of responsibility and compassion; the older generation refuse to accept guilt, seeing the working class as below them and wanting to focus on capitalist values of profit and personal gain; the younger generation resist guilt, linking to their upbringing, but eventually accept their wrongs; this shows hope for the future and the importance of breaking away from tradition and selfishness.

Answers

Grade	AO1 (16 marks)	AO3 (16 marks)	AO4 (8 marks)
6–7+	A convincing, well-structured essay that answers the question fully. Clear interpretation of a range of different aspects of the play. Quotations and references are well-chosen and integrated into sentences. The response covers the whole play.	Exploration is linked to specific aspects of the play's contexts to show a detailed understanding. Context is integrated with interpretation.	Consistent high level of accuracy. Vocabulary and sentences are used to make ideas clear and precise.
4–5	A clear essay that always focuses on the exam question. Some interpretation of different aspects of the play. Quotations and references support ideas effectively. The response refers to different points in the play.	References to relevant aspects of context show a clear understanding.	Good level of accuracy. Vocabulary and sentences help to keep ideas clear.
2–3	The essay has some good ideas that are mostly relevant. There is an attempt to interpret a few aspects of the play. Some quotations and references are used to support the ideas.	Some awareness of how ideas in the play link to its context.	Reasonable level of accuracy. Errors do not get in the way of the essay making sense.